Reversed Forecast

NICOLA BARKER

faber and faber
LONDON · BOSTON

First published in 1994
by Faber and Faber Limited
3 Queen Square London WC1N 3AU
This paperback edition first published in 1995

Typeset by Wilmaset Ltd, Wirral
Printed in England by
Clays Ltd, St Ives plc

A CIP record for this book is available
from the British Library

ISBN 0-571-17302-0

2 4 6 8 10 9 7 5 3 1

For Ben Thompson,
who's always liked a bit of a flutter

ONE

At night she breathed through her mouth, which would have been fine, if unerotic, except for the fact that her loose lips and sagging tongue spilled out copious quantities of saliva on to her pillow. Sometimes she woke up in the morning to find that the side of her mouth and chin, as well as portions of her lower cheek, had become damp and chapped from her sloppy expulsions.

She slept on her stomach – her breasts, soft pillows; her face, crushed against the bedclothes, misshapen by sleep, like the face of a pug, a boxer or a pekinese: inelegant but charming.

This morning – a Saturday – too, too early; she slept and she dreamed. In her dream she saw the wings of a large black bird. Some people are frightened by wings, she thought. And feathers. Some people are afraid of moths. The way they flutter. This fear – she didn't know the word for it – a nameless fear.

One instant the bird was at her shoulder, but the next it was outside her window, holding on to the sill with its strong claws, tapping, tapping.

Christ! she thought, suddenly feeling her body, her face, crashing into consciousness. Something *is* there at the window.

Ruby turned over and tried to open her eyes, both still gummed up with remnants of liquid eye-liner and mascara. She lifted a warm hand to wipe them clear, but this rapid movement, the whiteness of motion from her bleached hair, her pale skin, made the bird – if indeed it was a bird – fall from the sill, as though shot by an arrow of whiteness, a white lightning. When her eyes could properly focus, all she could see through her tiny bedroom window was a pinkish hue, reflected from wall to wall on the buildings outside – diluted light like a weak pink gin. She sniffed, still thinking of the bird. 'It was probably only a pigeon,'

1

she said, calming herself, then she opened her eyes wider, registered the reddish atmosphere outside and muttered, 'Bugger. It's going to rain.'

She turned over, relaxed, opened her mouth to inhale, and in a single breath was gone.

It didn't rain immediately. Several miles away a small dark woman stood alone on an open piece of roof-scape. She was still, rooted, like a tree, but her leaves were feathers, which quivered and vibrated in the slow, smouldering, morning light. The mass of birds on her outstretched arms were shrill, excitable, ecstatic, and called, *'Sylvia! Sylvia! Sylvia!'*

They were heavy, but Sylvia waited, remaining benign and impassive until one, last bird had arrived. It landed on her shoulder, gently brushing her cheek with its great black wing.

'Hello,' she said quietly, her voice low and rasping. 'I could see you coming from miles away. A minute ago you were only a tiny speck on the horizon.'

'Cor!' it replied, tipping its head, fixing her with a single, black eye.

She grinned and then dropped her arms, feeling the weight of many birds instantly lift, turning her head, hearing the whirrrr of their wings as she watched them ascend.

At ten-forty-five, Ruby ran across Wardour Street and made her way down towards the main bulk of the Berwick Street fruit market. Here she bought a bag of apples and smiled hello to various stallholders. She was late for work, but didn't seem concerned. From the far end of the market her peroxide hair was clearly visible amongst the bright cuts and smashes of different fruits – the casualty of colour.

To any incidental observer, standing attentive at the end of the market, watching out for motorbike couriers, the wasps, the fruit skins, Ruby painted a diverting picture.

She's bold, she's tall. When the men on the market call her a Big Girl, and they do, she spits out her tongue. Her short, unruly, badly bleached hair initially distracts attention from her large, red lips and black-lined eyes. She never tans, but she does wear tinted make-up to stop her skin from looking too pale, too insipid. She has a long nose which is rounded at the tip – not snub – and which suffers the indignity of a slight dent in the middle. She has a big but good body and her clothes are fashionable but not showy. (This is no place to be showy. Soho is cheap-showy.) She has green eyes and five hooped earrings in each ear. Until recently her nose was pierced too. On the palm of her right hand she has a tattoo, which depicts, somewhat clumsily, a small, blue bird in flight. This doesn't irritate her too much now – she tries not to regret things from the past – although sometimes it surprises her when she puts out her hand in shops to receive change.

Occasionally, as she walks, the market men send teasing whistles in her direction, which make her smile, check her tights and pull down her skirt. Her skirts are usually short but not excessively so, because her legs, although long, are also thick and muscular. If asked what part of her body she hated most, she would probably slap her thighs. She is resolutely curvy: a pear-shaped peach.

Close up, in focus, beyond the hair, the nose, the thighs, hides another essential, unmistakable, uncosmetic detail. It reveals itself physically, although it is not physical. It shows itself in her half-smiling, bright red, cherry lips. In her eyes, which see everything, are concerned with every small detail. You can hear it in her flat, soft voice. You can tell by the way she holds her arms, loose at her sides, informal and approachable. It hits you. It hurts you.

The main thing about Ruby is that she's obviously, un-ashamedly, determinedly *nice*.

Nice? And what does that mean?

One word. She laughs at it. *Trouble*.

Dawn was heaving a limp body through the shop doorway and swearing for all she was worth. Ruby paused and watched, unable to gain access while Dawn pushed and shoved. When Dawn paused for a second to draw breath, Ruby asked, 'What's he done wrong? He's just drunk. Leave the poor sod.'

Dawn frowned. 'Grab his feet will you?'

Ruby ignored her. 'What's he done?'

Dawn stepped over him and tried another angle, pulling now instead of pushing. He moved a couple more inches.

'He stinks. He's smelling out the fucking shop and he's putting off the punters.'

Ruby peered into the shop. It was empty. But what did that prove? It was still early. She bent over and perused the man's face more closely. She recognized him.

'I've taken bets off him before. He's not doing any harm. Can't you just leave him?'

'No.'

Ruby crouched down and tentatively nudged the man's shoulder. 'Come on, stand up and get out before she drags you out.'

He half-turned his head and grunted. His eyes were unfocused and he was drooling. She was uncertain what to do. Her impulse was to leave him alone, but Dawn was still pulling his feet from the other end. One of his shoes came off and she threw it into the street. It landed in a puddle next to the flower stall.

'Go on, Dawn, just leave him. It's still wet outside and he doesn't really smell.'

Dawn wasn't convinced. 'I've rolled him this far,' she said, 'and I'm not stopping here.'

The man began a half-hearted attempt to drag himself back into the shop, but collapsed after a couple of seconds. Ruby stood up, sighed, stepped over his body and left Dawn to it.

Jason, the manager, smiled at her through the glass partition and then stood up to unlock the door. He said, 'There's no stopping Dawn once she gets going.'

Ruby grimaced. She took off her coat and went into the back kitchen to make a cup of tea.

'Tea, Jason?'

'I only refuse blows.'

She plugged in the kettle. After a minute Dawn wandered in.

'Tea, Dawn?'

4

'Nah, I'm on the One-Cals today.' She opened the fridge and took out a can.

Ruby watched her. 'Were you early?'

She shrugged. 'Ten minutes. Jason was late. He'd only just opened up anyway.'

'I overslept again. I feel like hell.'

'You look like shit.'

Dawn opened her drink and flounced out, smirking.

Ruby waited for the kettle to boil. She felt bad about the dosser. When things like that happened they could undermine her whole day, and things like that happened all the time. She felt as though she hadn't had enough sleep, had a slight headache and wasn't happy at the notion of spending yet another day sitting by her till taking bets, helping Dawn with the clues in her crossword puzzle book.

The only positive aspect to working on a Saturday was the morning coverage of dog racing from Hackney. Sometimes, when she had a day off during the week, she worked as a kennel maid at the Hackney track, parading the dogs before their races and putting them into their traps. It was a good way of earning extra cash, and when Hackney was covered in the shops she had some familiarity with the dogs, the track and the personalities that worked there. It was, at least, a diversion.

The kettle came to the boil and switched itself off. She made the teas and strolled back into the shop just in time to see one of the punters – who was he? not a regular – approach the counter and smash his head into the glass partition next to the pay-out where Dawn had stationed herself and her can of One-Cal.

Ruby had long speculated whether the partition – which extended from the till to the ceiling with only a three-inch gap through which punters could push their betting slips and money – was glass or a type of reinforced plastic. This mystery was immediately resolved. The entire screen, whose purpose was to protect the working section of the shop (but chiefly the money), exploded into motion. It cracked, shattered and fell in a mixture of large random chunks and tiny, pebble-shaped splinters both inwards and outwards.

Ruby slammed down her hot drinks on Jason's desk and raised her arms over her head, protecting her eyes with her hands.

Jason had half-risen from his swivel chair, which spun behind him like a waltzer. A few of the smaller fragments of glass showered the back of his desk and nestled into the curls of his hair and moustache.

Initially, Dawn had thrown both hands forward, as if to catch the entire partition in her arms, but was now drawing them in again to protect her face and neck from the larger pieces which were descending from above.

Vincent (not a punter, not a regular; merely, for the time being, an aggressor) pulled his head back from the impact of the blow while his face composed itself into a violent snarl, which Ruby felt, in all probability, anticipated further damage. His forehead was cut directly below the hairline and blood was already pouring down to his eyebrows, through the funnel of his frown and on to the bridge of his nose.

After the few seconds of initial shock, Vincent began to scream obscenities at the three people standing behind the betting counter. By now his face was almost entirely awash with blood. Some of it ran on to his lips and into his mouth. He spat it out as he shouted, spraying out rude blood like an aerosol.

Jason ignored his yells and dialled the police. Ruby lowered her arms and glanced sideways at Dawn to check that she was all right. Then she turned towards Vincent. 'We're fine, but your head's all split.' Vincent squinted at her, surprised at being spoken to.

Jason placed his hand over the mouthpiece of the phone. 'Is anyone hurt? Dawn? Does he have a gun?'

Dawn shook her head. Small pieces of glass rattled down on to the carpet. She stood up. 'I don't think he's got a gun. He's too bloody stupid. If he'd had any brains, he'd have worked out that the side door's still open. He could've come straight in.'

She adjusted the collar on her blouse and then stalked off to the toilet.

Vincent had lost his initial impetus. Blood was streaming into his eyes. The first few punters of the morning were coming into the shop and standing around in clusters by the door. Jason picked up his keys and tossed them to Ruby. She caught them and made her way around the counter, encouraging everyone outside. 'Sorry. Looks like you're all going to have to find somewhere else to spend your money this morning.'

She grinned to herself. They were bound to close up for the day, and if she could get out quickly, she might be able to make it down to Hackney Wick in time for the second race. They always needed help on a Saturday.

When she closed the door she didn't lock it. Instead she walked over to Vincent and said quietly, 'Why don't you get out now while he's still on the phone? He's called the police and they'll be here any minute.'

Vincent glared at her. He looked like a red gargoyle. 'I don't need any favours from you.'

'Suit yourself.'

She walked back around the counter and into the kitchen, where she moistened one of the cleaner tea-towels in hot water, wrung it out, then returned to the shop and threw it at him. Vincent caught the towel and sank his face into it. Jason had finished with the police and was now deep in conversation with his area manager.

When Vincent lifted his head from the towel, Ruby noted that his face was square-shaped, with generous features but smallish eyes. It was a Celtic face – pale skin, reddish-brown lashes, stubble and brows – but his accent wasn't Irish or Scottish, only rough and vaguely rural. He was of medium build and stocky. Solid, she thought. And stupid. Like a ginger tom. She said, 'Some of our other shops don't have glass screens any more. Maybe you could go into one of those next time.'

He leaned up against the counter and appraised her. 'I was supposed to be meeting someone in here this morning, but I fell over him outside. He was lying in a pile of old fruit and cardboard. They told me on the stalls that you'd thrown him out.'

I didn't even do it, she thought; only let it happen.

'I didn't do it. Someone else did,' she said.

7

He blotted the towel against his forehead. 'Did you bother to take his pulse? Did you check he wasn't having a fit?'

Her eyes widened. 'He wasn't, was he?'

Vincent smiled. 'Who's to say?'

'He wasn't, was he?'

'Fuck you.'

The police arrived, pushed through the door and strolled in.

Ruby held out her hand to Vincent. 'My name's Ruby. I'll try to explain things if you like.'

Vincent slapped the damp, bloodied tea-towel down on her outstretched palm and said calmly, 'You'll pay for this.'

She backed off but was not afraid. She was tough enough. He was shorter than her by a couple of inches.

Oh yeah, she thought, walking back into the kitchen to make some more tea. Just another bad dream.

He left cuffed, but quietly.

TWO

When younger, Sylvia had been something of a diversion, a novelty, an idiosyncracy – eccentric but endearing. Now she's just a problem. And she knows it. She knows it well, but she doesn't care.

The general consensus on talent is that it is something that everybody appreciates, something that people want to share. Talent is just another commodity. No matter how obscure the talent may be, it's powerful, it's positive, it's something good.

Sylvia is nineteen. She thinks that she understands most things, and the things she doesn't understand she knows are of no interest to her. When she was fifteen she looked up the word 'talent' in her dictionary and saw that its origin was in the Greek *talanton*. The rough definition of this particular word was 'a weight'.

Talent, she decided, isn't always a good thing. It can't be. She pictured it as a weight around her neck, something heavy, choking and burdensome. She remembered Bette Davis in *Whatever Happened to Baby Jane?*

Sylvia is very ill, and it's all because of the birds. She suffers from a rare condition known as Bird Fanciers' Lung. This condition is caused by excessive contact with birds, their feathers and their dirt. Eventually you get allergic. Eventually it can kill you.

The first time Sylvia suffered symptoms of this rare disease was at the age of thirteen.

The birds had always loved her, she was always the apple of their beady eyes, but when she reached puberty (she reached it late and never seemed to get over the shock) the birds just couldn't resist her. She became a magnet for their tiny, fragile, feathery bodies. They simply couldn't bear to keep away.

And Sylvia grew to love them.

Her relationship with the birds isn't a silly or a dramatic one. She can't talk 'bird' for example; she certainly isn't a Dr Dolittle.

This makes her talent somewhat redundant. She can't put on a show with the birds – a circus show or a freak show. It is simply that they love her and she has grown to love them. Possibly the attraction is just hormonal – hormones are complex things – but possibly not.

Steven John had wasted a good part of the morning driving up and down Mare Street, Hackney, trying to locate the relevant turn off for Jubilee Road. He didn't know the area well and his sense of direction was abysmal. He'd tried perusing an old, dog-eared copy of the *A to Z*, but had been unable to work out which way up to hold it, which was left and which was right. Eventually he had managed, through sheer coincidence, to find the right road, the correct building and a handy parking space. The space, he thought; that at least must be a good omen.

Before getting out of his car he straightened his lapels and adjusted his collar.

He looked smart. His clothes were always of a high quality – hand cut – but slightly loud. He had a problem with colour. His suits were invariably too beige or too blue or too black. He usually wore a tie, a silk tie, and today was no exception. Peeking out from the inside pocket of his jacket was a gold-plated Parker pen and matching pencil. He found some difficulty in forming the letters correctly in real ink but preferred the classic charm of an ink pen to the bald, cheap brashness of its modern-day equivalent, the Biro. Biros, in his book, had no style and no class.

Steven John has always believed that the little things in life count. Sometimes he thinks that they count more than the big things. This small, almost mediocre philosophy of life is part of the reason why, in his own eyes, he has always been such an absolute failure. He feels insecure, lacks confidence and is devoid of panache. Even his name – this cuts him to the quick – is like two Christian names jammed gracelessly together. Of course it's a name that could easily be imagined on the front page of

Variety magazine. The kind of name someone on the cabaret circuit might have. The kind of someone who makes a break in the chorus of a West End musical. Probably homosexual.

It was as a consequence of his belief in the importance of detail that Steven resolved, at an early age, to gravitate towards the world of showbiz management. He was not made of the stuff of stardom, he knew this full well, but he was a pretender, a trier, a people person.

He sees himself as a fighter, an endurer, someone who battles manfully against all odds. The fact that he battles, suffers and invariably loses is incidental. He makes a living. Some people, he often thinks, correctly, can't even do that.

He entered the block of flats and, on discovering no lifts, began to climb the stairs. On reaching the third floor he became aware of a strong, musty flavour in the atmosphere – a smell akin to damp, but stronger. The brickwork was newly painted and the hallways seemed clean and well maintained. He put a hand to his throat and wished he was fitter, that his lean body was more athletic, so he wouldn't be compelled to breathe in this nastiness so deeply, so completely. He cleared his throat, although this didn't help matters, then continued his ascent.

The smell grew stronger as he reached the fifth floor. Restraining an impulse to sneeze, he raised his fist and rapped gently on the door of the top flat, which was painted a bright, fresh evergreen.

Within seconds the door was pulled open and Steven beheld Samantha, who was looking absolutely radiant and whose first response to his restrained nod of greeting was to smile and say, 'We thought you'd gone and stood us up.'

She took hold of his hand and shook it. Steven appreciated this small touch.

'Come in, we're just having breakfast. We were waiting for you, but it got so late we've already started.'

Her face was like a punch, a slap. She was so perfect that it set his teeth on edge. Like a madonna, a princess. Radiating something – an inexplicable serenity – from her black hair and her black eyes. Everything about her just so. A terrifying

11

neatness, a rightness. Her lips, a cupid's bow; her lashes, so long that he could have plucked them and used them to string a viola.

He forgot to say anything. He could have apologized for his lateness, but he found it impossible to contain anything else in his mind during that instant but her face – the glow of her. Words melted and turned into honey.

She led him through the flat. He followed, still numbed by her. If you had a relationship with a girl like this, he thought, you'd spend all your time trying to find some one thing wrong with her, and when you found it you'd be devastated.

Sam turned to say something to Steven as she led him along the corridor, and caught him staring at her bottom. She forgave him his indiscretion immediately, expecting no better than this from your average man. Steven blushed and continued to stumble down the corridor behind her, keeping his eyes to himself.

The flat was bright, clean and well decorated, but it stank. Steven couldn't understand the smell. He was momentarily worried that the smell might be his fault, and furtively checked the base of his shoes before following Sam into the kitchen.

The kitchen was painted a meticulous white and filled with red utensils. Sitting at a large red table in the centre of the room was Sam's mother, Brera, who was thirty-eight, had long auburn hair, fine features and slightly jutting teeth. She beckoned Steven towards the table without standing up. He found her grandly matriarchal.

The table was set with butter, jam, percolated coffee and a half-eaten plate of hot croissants. Steven noticed four settings and hesitated over where to sit. 'You've not gone to all this trouble on my account?'

Sam sat down on the chair to his left. 'Of course we have.'

She picked up a croissant and ripped it in two with her fingers. Steven sat down and nervously unfolded his napkin.

Brera poured him a cup of coffee. 'You're over an hour late, which is hardly an auspicious start.'

Sam grinned. 'Ignore her, she's only trying to frighten you.'

Steven felt daunted by these two women, both so vibrant and

voracious. So different. A black daughter, a white mother. Could you get more different than that? He picked up his coffee and placed it close to his nose so that its steamy aroma would cut out the smell of the flat which was starting to make him feel nauseous. He looked at Brera over the rim of his cup and said, 'I'm very pleased you agreed to meet up with me like this. When I saw the two of you last week at the Bull and Gate I was bowled over. It's not often you see two such attractive women on stage together who can actually sing, I mean really sing, let alone write their own music.'

Neither woman seemed especially impressed by this. Sam reached over for the coffee jug, scattering bits of pastry across the table in the process. She said, 'We've got lots of ideas, if that's what you mean.'

She poured her coffee and then licked her fingers clean. Steven watched her small pink tongue darting in and out of her mouth. It reminded him of a lizard's tongue or a hamster's. That's odd, he thought. I've never even seen a hamster's tongue before. He wondered why she had to talk, why she couldn't just sit. Just sit.

Brera said, 'Sam's in charge of this venture. She imagines everything, how we should be and so forth. She's fussy.'

Sam nodded. 'I am.'

Steven laced his fingers together. 'I can deal with that.'

'We've got a fairly pure vision. It's complex, but we can discuss all the details later.' Brera picked up a croissant and then spooned on some jam. 'We're bullies. We don't like being told what to do.'

Sam added, 'We've already decided that we won't put up with too many changes musically. We like doing some of our own stuff, well, my sister's stuff. We know it's eccentric . . .'

Steven began to look sceptical, but he kept in mind the fact that his latest client, a snooker player, had recently thrown in the towel to go back to his day job. He said, 'Obviously, the fact that you don't just do cover versions stands in your favour. Although my ideal image of the two of you is more as a mother-and-daughter soul and country duo. I prefer the country songs to the new-wave stuff.'

Sam mouthed the words 'new wave' at Brera and smiled. Steven was insulted. He thought, five years ago the term new wave was perfectly respectable.

Brera frowned at Sam and then said, 'Of course we'd be willing to consider some new songs for the act, so long as we don't lose all our own stuff.'

Sam leaned towards him and whispered, 'You think our own songs are crap, don't you?'

Before he could think how to respond she added, 'Well, that's OK, we think so too, sometimes. The problem is that they aren't written according to the standard musical scale.'

Brera interrupted. 'It's complicated, that's all.' Then she added, 'Don't worry, you'll soon get the hang of us.'

Steven was struggling to keep up. He said, 'So you both want me to manage you?' They nodded.

He felt as though he was missing out on something crucial, was bemused, but threw caution to the wind and said, 'Then I'd be delighted to.'

He held out his hand to Brera. Brera hesitated for a moment before taking it. She had the strong yellow nails of a long-time guitar plucker. After pressing his fingers for a second she let go and picked up the plate of croissants. 'Take one. They're nearly cold.'

Sam laughed. 'They *are* cold.'

Steven was secretly irritated that this courteous gesture on Brera's part had deprived him of the opportunity of shaking Sam's hand again. Sam didn't seem to care though. She was sipping her coffee and looking over at Brera as though they were sharing some kind of private joke. He hoped emphatically that he wasn't it.

Sylvia had been asked by both Sam and Brera to attend the breakfast meeting. She had agreed to go. 'After all,' they'd said, 'whatever the outcome, it's bound to affect you.'

She had agreed to go but had never had any real intention of attending, although this didn't dissuade her from standing outside the kitchen and listening to the on-going conversation inside. Occasionally she was forced to scamper back to her room to stifle her coughing, which was dry, hacking, and came in short bursts every few minutes.

She had watched Steven get out of his car and walk towards their block of flats from her window, and had disliked him, on principle, instantaneously. What she overheard from outside the kitchen didn't improve this opinion.

She was glad that she had kept out of the way. She was sure that her presence at the breakfast table would have spoilt the success of any joint venture.

Why should I care anyway? she thought furiously. I have my own bloody life.

She sat down on her bed and stared blankly at the carpet. She felt constricted. Things kept changing. Things always changed.

A sparrow flew in and landed on her shoulder. The pigeons cooed.

THREE

'How long have you been waiting?'

The policeman glanced at his watch. 'Five minutes.'

Ruby found him moderately attractive, for a policeman. He was tall but thin and had a deep dimple in either cheek and in his chin.

'I've come about the bail,' he said, stepping out of the doorway so she could get to her door.

'Why?' she said. 'What did I do?'

He smiled at this. While he smiled, it dawned on her. 'For *him*? You must be joking. He expects me to pay his bail?'

'He told me that you were the closest he had to a relative.'

Ruby's startled expression made him laugh out loud.

'You're just a sadist,' she said, 'in a bloody police uniform.'

'In case you wondered, I got your address from your manager. He said this was a company flat.'

Ruby felt around in the pocket of her jacket for her keys. 'I'm not paying his bail. I don't even know him.'

'That's up to you. He's got no money of his own.'

She put her key into the lock. 'I never even met him before today.'

'You must've made a good impression.'

'How much is it, anyway?'

'Two hundred.'

She pushed the door open. 'He can sing for it. You can tell him that.'

'I will.'

'Is that all?'

He nodded.

'Thanks, then.'

She stepped inside, then turned. 'Where is he exactly?'

'The local nick.' He began to grin. 'You're going to pay it, aren't you?'

'Even I,' she said firmly, 'am not quite that stupid,' and closed the door behind her.

Two hundred, she thought, climbing the stairs. He's crazy.

She'd almost reached the top when she heard the doorbell chime inside her flat. She swore, turned round, and walked back down again to answer it. Outside, instead of the policeman, whom she'd half-expected, was her friend Pablo. Everyone preferred to call him Toro. She didn't know why. He was holding two bottles of cheap lemon vodka. Ruby took a bottle from him and inspected the label. 'What's wrong with Martini or a crate of lager?'

Toro smiled, his cheeks bunched up and the pressure of them squeezed his eyes into almonds. 'I saw you at Hackney,' he said, 'on television.'

'Yeah?' She turned and started to walk upstairs again. 'Where? In Ladbrokes? How did I look?'

He slammed the front door and followed her. 'Completely beautiful.'

'Thanks.'

Once inside, Ruby took off her jacket and slung it over the back of the sofa, then flung herself into an armchair and scraped her heels across the floor to pull off her shoes. She wriggled her stockinged toes and said, 'Maybe I should grow my toenails and paint them, then I could wear sandals and my feet wouldn't sweat as much.'

Toro looked slightly disgusted. 'Why was the shop closed this morning?'

She didn't answer immediately, so he searched for the volume percentage of alcohol on the label of one of the bottles he was holding.

Ruby's flat was comfortable but shoddy. It consisted of a small sitting-room and adjoining kitchen, with an old Baby Belling, a sink and a fridge, a tiny bathroom and a small box-shaped bedroom. The walls were painted a uniform creamy yellow which gave the place a distinctly institutional feel. The furniture was old but solid. Ruby had few homely or ornamental posses-sions, but a lot of clothes and records. The records lined one wall of the sitting-room and items of clothing, clumps of accessories and numerous pairs of boots and shoes had been tossed about with general disregard. The room was dusty.

Toro unscrewed the top of a vodka bottle and asked for some glasses. Ruby picked up a couple of dirty mugs and went to the sink to give them a wash. She couldn't find a clean tea-towel to dry them with so used a bathroom towel instead. Toro grimaced at them. 'The mouth of these mugs is too thick.'

'Not mouth, lip. You should know. You're the wine waiter.'

She banged the mugs on to the floor next to his feet and sat down again while he poured. He half-filled both mugs and then handed her one. She took a sip, pulled a face, but said nothing. Two hundred quid, she thought.

Toro was over fifty and poorly though smartly dressed in a grey suit and old shirt. He was small and slightly overweight, with dark black hair, greased back, and sallow cheeks. His eyes were hooded, red, but lively. She'd never seen him clean-shaven, but often smelled aftershave on him – a whiff of cinnamon and spearmint. He worked in a restaurant, but spent most of his time gambling.

Ruby told him about Vincent and he listened intently. She concluded, 'I've never even met him before, but now he expects me to fork out two hundred in bail money.'

'That Dawn's a bitch.'

Ruby wasn't receptive to this. She didn't want to feel impli-cated. Even so, she said, 'I've still got the money I won on the National. I've got at least two hundred left. I wanted to use it for something sensible, to invest it . . . I dunno.'

Toro bent over and screwed the top back on the bottle. 'You were lucky for me this morning. I bet on the two dogs you were with at Hackney. Won both times.'

He indicated the two bottles with a smile. Ruby smiled too; not at him, but to herself.

'They were Donald Sheldon's dogs,' she said. 'He came over and had a chat. He said he'd offer me a job full-time if he got the chance. Took my number and everything. I told him I'd sooner be a trainer than a kennel-girl. Lots of women do it, you know.'

Toro chuckled. He said, 'A big dog in a place like this?'

She scowled. He offered her the bottle again. She gulped down her vodka in one go and passed him her cup. While he poured she visualized Donald Sheldon. Top trainer at Hackney, she thought, remembering how he'd put his hand on her arm as he'd spoken to her. Creepy. Sexy. Too old for me, and too flash.

Toro was watching her face. 'Don't pay that bail,' he said, misinterpreting her thoughtful expression.

'What?'

'He's taking you for a fool.'

She stood up and went into the kitchen, took a coffee jar out of the cupboard, opened it and removed a bundle of notes.

'Toro,' she said, suddenly feeling lively and quite purposeful.

'What?'

'You're full of bull.'

In the bathroom, she applied a thick coat of bright red lipstick, licked her teeth to ensure it hadn't smudged on them, stared into the mirror at her own simple, stupid face, and mouthed the word *moron*.

FOUR

Sam was peering through the kitchen window, trying to see if Steven was outside yet and what kind of car he drove. Brera was clearing the table. Sam said, 'He drives an old Jag. I wonder what that means.'

Brera piled a cup on to a plate, a cup on to a plate, a cup on to a plate. Spinal column, she thought, vertebra, disc, vertebra, disc. She carried them carefully over to the sink, slipped them into the soapy water and then peered out too. 'Your problem,' she said curtly, 'is that everything always has to mean something. I like him.'

'That's simple enough,' Sam said, wondering what Brera meant exactly.

Steven was debating whether it would be possible to get an old girlfriend of his to do some promotional shots of the Goldhawk Girls. (Bad name, he thought. That'll be the first thing to go.) She wasn't professional, but she was cheap.

As he drew closer to his car, he noticed that the side mirrors had been pulled off and that the aerial had been twisted into a heart shape. 'Curse the bastard,' he muttered. 'Curse the bastard that did this.' He grabbed the aerial and tried to straighten it.

Sylvia walked out of her room and into the kitchen. 'He makes me want to spew,' she announced.

Sam and Brera were doing the washing up. They both turned to look at her.

'He liked your songs,' Sam lied. 'You should've come in and said hello.'

Sylvia removed a strand of her hair from the confines of the pony-tail she was wearing and twisted it around her finger. 'He hated the songs. I heard him.'

Brera pulled out a chair and sat down. 'He thought they were good but unusual.'

'Don't make me laugh.'

Brera crossed her arms and stared at Sylvia as she stood in the doorway. 'Grow up.'

'I'm nineteen. That's old enough.'

For what? She didn't look nineteen. She looked twelve. Like a scruffy, ill-adapted pre-teen.

'And by the way,' she added, 'I vandalized his car.'

Brera continued to stare at her. 'You appal me.'

Sam leaned on the window-sill and peered out again. Steven was still there, yanking at his aerial.

'It's only the aerial,' she said. 'Anyway, it's an old car.'

Sylvia glared at her. 'Who asked you?'

Brera threw herself forward on to the table and banged her forehead against it. *Thump*. She did it again. *Thump*.

Sylvia was furious. 'Stop it!'

Brera stopped and straightened up. 'Are you happy now?'

'Yes!' Sylvia shouted, and the shout turned instantly into a cough, into several coughs, whooping coughs.

She couldn't breathe. She clutched her stomach and leaned against the side of the door, bent double.

Good, she thought. Punishment for everybody.

She coughed carelessly, loosely, so that the unrestrained force of her hacking might rip up her throat and bring out blood. She visualized the cough as two tiny beings playing volleyball inside her throat, passing the tickle back and forth, catching it, returning it, blocking it, holding it. If only, she thought desperately, seeing their impassive faces through her streaming eyes, if only they could enjoy my illness as much as I do.

She turned, still coughing, and staggered back down the corridor.

'Go!' Brera shouted after her. 'I'm sick of the sight of you!'

Sam began washing up again. After a minute or so she said, 'I think she feels left out.'

21

Brera rubbed her eyes. 'She's such a little bitch. She never does anything for herself and she resents everything we do.'

Sam ran a finger across the bubbles in the sink, watched them burst on her skin. 'She's bound to feel threatened by Steven. She might feel like she's losing us. Losing something.'

Brera's lips tightened. 'To hell with what she thinks.'

Sam glanced towards the open door and then walked over to shut it. As she turned back she said, 'Perhaps we should've explained about her to Steven. I'm sure he would've understood, and if he hadn't, then we wouldn't have wanted anything to do with him anyway.'

'You think I'm ashamed of her?'

Brera's eyes filled. Sam found the sight of her mother's imminent tears disagreeable and unsettling. I shouldn't feel that way though, she decided, and tried not to. She pulled off a piece of kitchen roll and handed it to her. Brera blew her nose and then looked up. Her eyes were bloodshot.

'I'm frightened, that's all. I want to protect her.' Her eyes exuded tears: large, fat tears like transparent slugs, slithering down her face. 'She's such a little shit.'

Sam watched the tears. If I taste one, she thought, then everything will be all right. She put out her hand and brushed a tear from Brera's chin on to her finger, then let it fall from her finger on to the end of her tongue.

'She'll be fine,' she said.

FIVE

Vincent had been staring at his hands with unswerving concentration for almost five hours. During this time there had been no perceptible change in their appearance.

After his initial statement to the two police officers – 'I fell over. I banged my head' – a short period of speculation about bail payments and a perfunctory medical check, he had refused to involve himself in any further interaction. This hadn't really worked to his advantage, but he hadn't honestly expected it to.

Within the previous couple of weeks he had been detained on two occasions and charged on one of these for breach of the peace. He was hardly a novice in the cells, and, as such, no one paid him much attention.

While he stared at his hands his mind ran over a variety of subjects. *Larson. Arson. Willie Carson.* Occasionally he slumped into an unthinking daze, but when he came to and refocused on his dirty nails, fingers and the pale hair on the back of his knuckles, his mind raced on with as much enthusiasm as if it had never paused. *Blood in my nostrils, dried blood, like paint.*

He often lost all track of time. His life was a strange mixture of time-using (demonstration) and time-wasting (remonstration).

He has many opinions, his own opinions, and he has many faults. The chief one is intolerance. He sees himself as an anarchic bob-a-job man – doing favours, splitting hairs, trading down. Always down. He is unusual in that his intolerance and his pureness of vision haven't made him into boot-boy, a Tory or a fascist. He is the opposite of these things; is ceaselessly, peacelessly contrary.

My life. What fucking life? No life. Low life.

He has a terror of involvement, of commitment – to places, to things. He won't be held culpable or responsible, will only represent one view: his own view. He thinks the world, everything, is stupid.

Stupid!

During the course of his twenty-nine years, he has never seen any purpose in dedicating himself to traditionally worthy or helpful occupations. He refuses to give over his considerable powers to anything specifically useful. His prime, twin attributes of determination and energy have never been expressed constructively. If they are – and of course he thinks that they are – he has a definition of 'constructive' which is all his own.

He survives on a diet of grand gestures, obnoxiousness and guile.

Only one thing blots his anarchic copy-book. It is a simple thing. He is full of love. So full of love – indiscriminate, luminous, pulsating, unremitting – that it threatens to make him weak, to make him burst, to make him give in, completely. To what, though? He doesn't know.

The strange thing about love, Vincent decided, studying the white flecks on the pink moons of his nails, is that it starts off as one thing, and comes out as something altogether different.

His arresting officer pushed open the cell door and walked in. 'Your bail's been settled.'

I love this man, Vincent thought, but it'll come out some other way.

He looked up from his hands. 'Fucking bail. What a joke.'

'Yeah, very funny.'

He stood up. 'Can I go?'

'Sign a couple of papers and you're a free man, for the time being, anyway. So long as you don't behave like a lunatic again before your court case.'

Vincent smiled. 'Well, that's hardly too much to ask for, is it now?'

When he caught sight of Ruby she was leaning against the reception desk reading a pamphlet about the police cadets. She looked up as the door swung back and slammed behind him. He thought, My God, she's a push-over. The best kind of girl.

He pulled on his canvas jacket and said, 'You can get me something to eat if you like.'

Ruby picked up the pamphlet and stuffed it into her pocket. 'I don't think so.'

His eyes, she noticed, were like two blue marbles. He adjusted the collar on his jacket, grinned at her and strolled outside. Ruby nodded to the constable behind the reception desk and followed him.

She stepped into the afternoon sunlight and saw him disappearing into a burger bar over the road. She crossed cautiously and followed him in. He beckoned to her from the counter. 'How about buying me a burger and a drink?'

'Why should I?'

'Because you're loaded.'

She scowled at him. 'How did you work that one out?'

'I want a burger, a Coke and some chips.'

The counter girl flinched at the mention of the word 'chip' and then looked to Ruby for her order. Ruby sighed. 'I'll have a medium coffee please, with cream.'

Vincent sauntered off and took possession of a plastic table next to the window. Ruby paid, and while she waited for the order, counted the remaining small coins in her purse. Vincent was sitting at the table and running his fingers over the cut on his hairline. The cut stretched across a bluish lump and glimmered like a red mouth. Ruby supposed that he must have been given a stitch, although it didn't look like it from where she was standing.

Her order arrived. She picked up her tray and made her way to the table. Vincent looked up at her. 'I haven't eaten all day.'

She sat down, removed her coffee and then pushed the tray towards him. She felt light-headed.

'Your hands aren't very clean. I don't think you should touch that cut. It might get infected.'

He shrugged. 'I've had worse. It's given me one hell of a headache, though. I could do with a proper drink.'

'Maybe you're concussed. What did the doctor say?'

'I don't know. Some crap. I might get gangrene of the brain.'

He was joking. Ruby gently removed the lid from her polystyrene cup. You've already got it, mate, she thought.

He noticed the tattoo on her hand. 'What's that? A name? A bird?'

'A swallow. I did it when I was seventeen.'

He wiped some ketchup from the side of his mouth with the back of his hand. 'Let's see.'

She opened her palm and showed him.

'You did it yourself?'

She nodded. 'Pen and a pin.'

'Ouch.'

She sipped her coffee. 'What did you tell the police?'

'I told them I tripped.'

'Did they believe you?'

'No.'

'Was your friend all right? The epileptic.'

'I only met him once before.'

'What do you mean?'

'He wasn't my friend.'

Ruby tried to understand this, but had trouble doing so.

'Was he an epileptic?'

'Might be. He didn't say he wasn't.'

'He was unconscious.'

'Exactly.'

She said, 'You're not from London, are you?'

'Why?'

'You don't sound like you are.'

'Nope.'

'Where are you staying?'

He thought for a while. 'Wembley.'

'Really?'

'On someone's floor. Before that I was in Amsterdam. Squatting.'

She visualized him, squatting, in a field full of tulips. A windmill.

He was eating his fries and his fingers were greasy. He said, 'In case you're wondering, I'm not naturally a violent person.'

She smiled at this. She could see no reason to deny being violent unless you actually were violent. He noticed her smile and was indignant. 'Give me some credit.'

'Two hundred quid,' she answered, 'that should do you.'

He continued to eat in silence. Eventually she said, 'Will I get it back?'

He thought about this for a while. 'You shouldn't have paid it.'

'I thought I'd get it back.'

He offered her one of his fries and she shook her head. 'What were you planning to do with it?'

She shrugged. 'I dunno. Save it.'

He squinted at her. 'Well, saving it isn't doing anything.'

'I was going to do something.'

'What?'

She tried to think. 'Something. An investment. I don't want to discuss it.'

'Why not?'

'It's private.'

'You could give it to charity.'

'Haven't I already?'

He gulped down his Coke and then licked his teeth. 'It's kind of like . . .' he said thoughtfully, 'I'm your investment.'

He was pleased by this. He couldn't imagine a worse investment. And I'm me, he thought. Fuck only knows how she feels about it. He chuckled to himself.

She drank some more of her coffee. With her free hand she felt underneath the table, touched something soft, instinctively stuck her nail into it and then realized that it was chewing gum. She quickly withdrew her hand. The table was a startlingly bright yellow. All along its edge were melt marks, brown stains from cigarettes.

'I was going to invest it properly,' she said, after a pause, 'in a small business.'

'Two hundred,' he said. 'That'll get you a long way.'

'I was intending to.'

'I bet you were.'

She glared at him. She dealt with men like him every day at

work. One day, she knew for sure, she would do something constructive and she wouldn't have to deal with men like him any more.

She turned and looked out of the window, into the street. She saw pigeons, people, grey buildings. This city, everything in it, including me, is a big lump of grey muck, she thought.

'I've got a headache now,' he said. 'Do you live near here?'

'Why?' She stared at him again.

'I only wondered.'

'Why?'

'I just need to put my head down for half an hour.'

She started to laugh. I'm pissed, she thought. I'd rather die than invite him home.

Eventually she said, 'You think I'm a bloody push-over.'

'You are.'

She was.

Sylvia's room always seemed dark, although it had no curtains and the windows were usually open. The walls, which had once been white, were now a shabby grey. Bits of wallpaper hung in strips where the birds had ripped at it to secure lining for their nests.

No attempt had been made to clear up the splatterings of dirt left by the birds on the floor, or at the bases of the thirty or so perches which had been erected on three of the four walls. Here it had formed into small, pointed, pyramidic piles.

The perches varied in size and were nailed to the wall in a series of regimented lines. They were fixed at four heights, some ten or so inches from the floor, others only inches from the ceiling. They encroached on the room, making it seem much closer and smaller than it actually was. About a quarter of the perches had been enlarged and built into perfunctory nesting boxes, although the birds rarely hatched their eggs or brought up their young within the room's perimeter.

Pushed up against the only clear wall was Sylvia's bed. The duvet was a dark green colour, stained intermittently by whitish bird droppings. There was little else in the room except for a large, grey trunk at the foot of her bed in which she kept all her clothes and the few other personal possessions that she valued.

The room was rarely quiet. The air was constantly full of the sound of vibrating wings, of bird argument and intrigue, and underneath each sound, humming at the very bottom, the purring, cooing, singing of the pigeons.

Wild birds are not naturally aromatic creatures, but the consequence of a large number of them inhabiting an enclosed space was that the room smelled something like a chicken coop. It was a strong and all-pervasive smell which was gradually taking over the top few floors of the block. During fine weather – in the heat – the smell expanded and could be detected over an even wider area.

Sylvia was oblivious to the smell. Since she rarely ventured out of the flat, it never struck her as out of the ordinary. Sometimes she noticed it when she travelled back indoors from her dawn vantage point on the roof, but even then it smelled like something good and reliable, a heavy, dusty, musty familiarity.

She knew that the dirt, the smell and the feathers were bad for her. Often she tasted this in her mouth after she had coughed. When she suffered from an asthma attack she would use her inhaler and hide under her duvet, somehow believing that the air under here was cleaner, free of the cloying thickness.

During the long, solitary periods spent in her room, Sylvia usually sat on the trunk at the foot of her bed with her legs drawn up and her chin resting on her knees.

She did very little, but was skinny. Her face was not thin, though. It was round and her cheeks were pouched and protuberant. Her father was a Cypriot. She had never met him, never mentioned him. Her mouth and nose were heavy and her lids and lips were thick and rich. Her eyes were a bright deep green: ironic cat's eyes.

Most people – apart from those who were expert in such matters – presumed her to be retarded. Yet it always grew increasingly difficult (with familiarity) to pinpoint exactly how this was. She was numerate, literate, articulate. Only her will was retarded. She couldn't quite do anything. She couldn't quite want anything. She had no real desire, except to be left alone. She didn't even really want the birds that much, but she perceived them as though they existed in a different realm of being, a realm of necessity, of inevitability.

Earlier on, Brera had supposed that external stimuli might renew Sylvia's vigour, her will. She had tried psychotherapy, counselling, family therapy. But nothing had worked. Nothing encroached. She remained aloof.

Sometimes Sylvia sat in her room and with a great deal of effort tried to summarize her life, to get her head around its totality. Whenever she did this, she could think only of nothing. Of a vacuum. The enormity of this vacuum terrified her. So instead she fixed things in terms of the birds, in a feathery cycle of birth, youth, age, death. This meant that after a time she couldn't actually do without them. They were her.

Straight after the argument she had regretted it. Steven John didn't really matter, she knew that. He didn't threaten her. He couldn't change things.

She sat on her trunk, pressed her chin into her knees and thought, I want them to leave me. I want things to be quieter and simpler. If they deserted me, if they grew tired of me, I could sit here for ever. I wouldn't have to try any more and that would be good. I think that would be good.

She knew it.

Because he had forced himself to await a precise time before calling on her, Steven felt almost as though a previous arrangement had been made for this meeting. He felt confident. He waited for her to say something as he stuck his thumb into his belt and grinned.

Ruby squinted out at Steven through the half-light, her expression a mixture of impatience and exhaustion. 'Oh God.'

His expression sank from cheerful to jowlful. 'I'm pleased to see you too,' he said.

He watched as she pushed her hand through her hair. He thought, She's still wearing too much make-up and her skirt is too tight. Paradoxically, these familiar flaws made him feel inexplicably fond.

'Can I come in?'

'Um.' She thought about this for a moment. 'Why don't we go out for a drink? I can run up and fetch my coat.'

'And put some shoes on.' He pointed to her stockinged feet.

'Yeah.' She turned. 'Wait here.'

He ignored this and followed her, up the stairs and into her flat.

Her jacket was slung over the arm of a chair. She grabbed it and frantically looked around for her shoes. He stood in the doorway and appraised the room, wondering what it could be that she was so keen to conceal. Someone was in the bathroom. He could hear a tap running. She pulled on a pair of boots. 'That's Toro,' she said, 'washing his face.'

'Why?'

'He's drunk. He won on a couple of races this morning.'

Steven stared at the bathroom door, waiting for it to open.

She checked in her pocket for her keys. 'Right, let's go.'

'Don't you want to tell him?'

'What?'

'That you're going out.'

She stood in front of him, awkwardly, her eyes unblinking, hiding something. 'No.'

He looked not at her but over her shoulder.

'How about that person on the floor?'

'Who?'

She turned. 'Oh. Him. He's fine.'

Vincent lay on his back, spread-eagled across the carpet, his head hidden from view behind the sofa.

'Is he sleeping or what?'

She sighed. 'It's not a problem.'

Before he could respond to this she said, 'How do you manage to always make me feel so bloody guilty?'

He shrugged. He just had that knack. They both knew the reason. He disapproved of her. He liked her, but he thought her capable of behaving, at times, stupidly and carelessly. She allowed her life to become sordid. He found this hateful.

He walked over to where Vincent lay. 'Who is he? Do I know him?'

'No.'

'Is he all right?'

'I think so. He passed out.'

'When?'

'Five minutes ago.'

'His head's disgusting.'

'He did it this morning.'

'He must be concussed. Has he been drinking?'

She smiled, unhappy. 'He got shit-faced with Toro. One minute he was chatting away, the next, pop! Flat out.'

'Is he breathing?'

Ruby stepped across Vincent's prone body and lifted one of his eyelids to reveal the white of his eye. 'He's out cold.'

She stood up again.

'You aren't just going to leave him there?'

'Yes, I am.'

Some things she'd always disliked about Steven. He liked order and he didn't often do dirty or grubby things. She believed that he thought them, but he wouldn't do them, wouldn't let them happen. So he disapproved of her for letting them happen. And I do, she thought, I really do.

Toro staggered out of the bathroom, barely acknowledging them both, stumbled into the living-room and sat down on the sofa.

'I'll meet you in the pub,' Steven said, his tone measured. 'The Blue Posts.'

'Right. Give me five minutes.'

There's a line, he thought, heading down the stairs, a fine line between being soft and being stupid. She can't see it.

It was a moral flaw. He believed this. But morality didn't interest him, only manners.

Ruby wandered into her bedroom to find a blanket. After a short, fruitless search she pulled one from her bed and carried it into the sitting-room. She wondered whether it was preferable to let Toro stay or to make him go home, but by the time she'd returned with the blanket that decision had already been made. Toro was stretched out on the sofa, covered in his coat, fast asleep and snoring.

She looked down at her wrist-watch. It was only eight-thirty. She made her way over to where Vincent lay and covered him with the blanket. She touched his hand, which felt stiff and cold, so she knelt down next to his head and put her ear close to his mouth. His breath touched her ear and tickled it.

She turned her head to stare at him. His face was tense, even in sleep. He was frowning. She inspected the skin on his cheeks very closely: the pores, the paleness and the small, reddish bristles of his beard. Her eyes were drawn to the bump on his forehead which now appeared much angrier and tighter than before, and the cut, much purpler. A few of the hairs in his fringe had bent down into the mouth of the cut. She repressed the desire to move them, to pull them out, in case this should wake him.

She moved back a fraction, still staring. He looked gruff but intelligent. He seemed troubled. She thought, I wonder what he does? She had a suspicion that he didn't do anything.

She frowned and then pulled the blanket up and tucked it around his chin.

Steven had already bought her a drink.

'Thanks.'

She took it from him and sipped it. She had known him for six months. He was her oldest friend in London. He'd lived in London all his life. He was an expert at it. She'd arrived six months previously from Sheffield. They'd met at night-school on a photography course.

'Would you do me some photos?' he said.

She grimaced.

They'd bought a camera together, during their single month of intimacy. She'd kept it. He liked borrowing it. Borrowing her. Will he ask about Vincent? she wondered. Will he moan about Toro? Steven knew Toro of old and hated him. Not so much hates, she decided, just doesn't have the time.

'If we arrange it for Tuesday,' he said, 'that'd be good. Four, half-four.'

The ceiling, she noted, was stained beige with smoke. In centuries to come, she thought, scientists will find this ceiling and they'll have the equipment to analyse the smoke, to tell something about the lives of every single person that ever exhaled in this pub.

Ruby. Unnatural blonde. Never wore matching underwear. A pushover.

'Hang on,' he said, 'make it five, to be on the safe side.'

Steven. Big hands. Nice face. Small ears. Gives Ruby a hard time.

Steven wrote down the address. 'They're called Sam and Brera. Brera's Irish. You'll like them.'

He handed her the slip of paper. 'Don't lose it.'

She frowned at him.

'Yeah, well, I know how you are.'

She recognized several people in the pub. Punters. Where do they get their money from? she wondered. Not from me. Losing's the whole point of a gamble.

34

'Be professional,' he said, slightly embarrassed to be asking. 'Take the tripod and everything. Also, this might sound stupid, but, well, try and ignore the smell.'

She tried to remember the last time she'd had a bath. Last night? Yesterday morning?

'Did Toro go?'

She shook her head. Here it comes, here it comes. I'm stupid, I'm useless.

As he spoke she wove a fantasy out of different parts of the pub's decor: the colour of the liquor in the bottles, the texture of the barman's starched, white shirt. In this fantasy, she was very rich, she did what she liked. No one told her what to do.

SEVEN

Vincent opened his eyes. Black. He turned his head to try to look around him. It was then that he realized that he had no head. He didn't attempt to confirm or deny this possibility by touching his face. He said, 'If I have no head, how can I touch my face?' and then, 'God, my voice sounds strange. Where's it coming from? My armpit? My arse?' Wouldn't be the first time, he thought.

After a moment's consideration he said, 'Why am I talking out loud? Maybe I'm not talking at all. Maybe all this darkness is only inside me. Fuck.'

He staggered to his feet and banged his leg against the stereo. It rattled. The room wasn't completely dark, but even so, he still had some trouble locating objects and moving without collision.

He veered away from the stereo and smacked into the back of the chair. He paused and stared fixedly in front of him, making out the blurred shape of the sofa and a lump on it which seemed like a sleeping figure. Slowly he recalled Toro, although he had forgotten his name. Shortly after he remembered that he was in Ruby's flat. I did it! he thought. That was a result.

He made his way towards the left-hand side of the sofa, moved around it and located the small kitchen work surface with his right hand. He felt blindly for the sink, turned on the tap, then fixed his lips to the bright, white stream of water that poured from it. He drank for a few seconds and felt the water rush through his mouth and throat to his stomach and then through his temples where it banged and pounded.

His head rematerialized. It began to hurt. He touched it and it felt hot. His hand discovered the lump on his hairline and it surprised him. He touched the lump again, very gently, then muttered, 'How come I saw the water when I couldn't see hardly anything else? I must be able to see everything.'

He looked around him again and immediately the room was quite clear.

He decided to go and study his lump more closely in the bathroom, although he couldn't remember exactly where it was. He didn't relish the prospect of stumbling into Ruby's bedroom.

Luckily both doors were ajar. Vincent couldn't resist the temptation to peer around the door into Ruby's room, and when he did was surprised to see that it was empty.

Suddenly he felt an intense urge to urinate. He grabbed at the buttons on his trousers and rushed to the toilet. He produced very little liquid and felt vaguely dissatisfied, but before he was able to locate this dissatisfaction, a blast of nausea hit his throat and threw him forward, towards the toilet bowl. In a matter of seconds he had reproduced mashed burger, sloshy fries, a substance not unlike popcorn – my spleen, he thought – and a mouthful of phlegm.

He was shaking. He was desperate. He crawled into Ruby's room and climbed on to her bed. The blankets were in a state of disarray. He forgot to remove his shoes.

Brera ate a yoghurt in front of the television and worried about Sylvia. She had gone out a few hours earlier and had not yet returned.

It was eight-thirty. Brera rarely went out on a Saturday night. She had rarely gone out any night before the Goldhawk Girls. Sam, however, was excessively sociable.

When Sam was away, Sylvia and Brera would sit in front of the television and watch whatever was on in companionable silence. Sylvia didn't actually watch. She always kept her eyes closed. Brera supposed that this was because she had no interest in television, but the truth was that Sylvia had become too sensitive. She could either listen or watch, but she couldn't manage both. She couldn't cope with the noise of television – the conflict of voices, music, slogans – while taking in its speedy visual menu of flashing colours, signs and faces. It overwhelmed her, but she realized that she and Brera had little else in common except the television – sitting in front of it, together.

37

Brera picked a raspberry pip from between her teeth. She knew that Sylvia's trip out was a form of protest, but she didn't want to consider Sylvia's motivation too fully, couldn't risk feeling implicated.

Instead of wondering why she'd gone, she wondered where she'd gone. This seemed an altogether simpler proposition.

The act of walking with purpose and the elimination of her usual close environment made Sylvia's inhalation easier and reduced her coughing. She was in the process of considering this fact when, just after six-thirty, she made her way briskly down to the canal. She intended to follow it to Victoria Park. She fancied seeing the ducks.

On Saturday evenings the canal was usually chock-a-block with fishermen. Each sat in a solitary daze, focusing only on the water. Each resented the presence of others, resented the casual purposelessness of the average stroller.

Sylvia kept her head down on her way to the canal, through the complex assortment of streets that led from the flat to the water's edge. But it was dusk, a quiet time. Most people were at home by now. Most birds were thinking about roosting.

She reached the canal in good time, but before following its curvaceous route to the park, she paused on its brink and stared at herself in the black, polluted water. Her face shimmered as a tiny fish swam under the surface and breathed a bubble of oxygen to the top.

The canal was silent and eerie. For the first time since leaving the flat she felt fully a sense of the hugeness of her environment. She envied the birds their more acute understanding of space, their capacity to fill it and use it.

She turned and began to walk. Her eyes watched her own feet, the beginning of each step and its completion. The pathway was covered in a golden gravel substance which threw up a light dust in front of her and behind her. The old sandals she wore gave it access and she felt it settle between her toes.

The rhythm of walking calmed her. It made her mind empty itself of all things except the single task of consuming distance.

The birds were rarely a problem when she walked at this time of day. Had it been earlier, they might have flocked, massed and pestered her, but in the late afternoon they were dozy and dazy. Just the same, she thought it best to move rapidly, quietly and to stare at her feet.

When she had covered a good three-quarters of the route, her concentration was interrupted by a small group of boys who were hunched in a bundle by the edge of the river. One of them was passing a fishing net to and fro in the water. As she walked by, the boy with the net looked up and stared at her. He was a mean-faced child of eight or ten – thin, petulant and aggressive. Sylvia sensed him watching her. She walked until she was directly adjacent to him and then caught his eye. This was foolish. He grinned and said, 'You've got a face like a pig. You look like a monkey. You're stupid.'

She continued walking, her eyes returning to the ground. She sensed the other boys staring at her too, their eyes making the skin on her back crawl. One of them (larger than the others) said, 'She's from a funny farm. She's an old woman. She's got no tits.'

The other boys laughed in unison and then pored over the net to see if anything was caught in its mesh.

Sylvia flinched but did not falter. She walked on determinedly, reached the park and entered it through its grand wrought-iron gates. The benches in the park had been painted an ostentatious blue and gold. She sat down on one which was close to the lake. Everything felt too big. She stared at the lake through a tangle of hair that had formed into a long fringe over the top half of her face.

A tiny finch fluttered down from a nearby tree, landing on the back of the bench, only a few inches from her. Sylvia noticed the bird, but did not move her head or body towards it, only her eyes. They stared at one another and then Sylvia's eyes returned to the lake, which looked still and grey-green. Its surface was dotted with pieces of white fleecy down – feathery remnants. She wondered absent-mindedly whether the geese had been fighting or moulting.

The finch pecked at her T-shirt, trying to procure himself a

39

strand of fabric. Sylvia offered him her index finger. He jumped on to it. She felt the tiny weight of him and watched the breeze ruffle the millionfold feathers on his chest. His feet were scratchy and dry. They itched the eczema on her hands. She moved him closer to her face and whispered, 'Hello Dry-foot. Hello Dry-foot.'

The bird blinked, cocked his head and then reached up and grabbed hold of a single strand of her hair. He jerked it from her scalp. Sylvia laughed, and the sound of her voice propelled him skyward.

The park was quiet. Fifteen yards to her left she noticed a young girl and a woman standing by the lake's edge. The girl was eating a sandwich. She looked about five years old. The woman, who Sylvia presumed to be the child's mother, bent down to talk to her and then walked away. Sylvia decided that she must be going to the seafood stall on the park's perimeter. She frowned and thought, That girl looks too young to be left alone. Everything's big. There are so many possibilities. None of them good.

Her attention was distracted by a tatty flotilla of Canada geese who were gradually making their way towards the edge of the lake. She stood up, pushed some hair behind her ears and strolled over to them. They crowded around the bank as Sylvia squatted down and smiled at them. A couple of them honked their admiration. She reached out a slow hand and rubbed the edges of the closest bird's beak. This was a form of caress that most birds usually understood.

As she petted the geese Sylvia noticed that the girl was moving towards her. She was small and skinny with wide blue eyes and yellow curls. She sidled up to Sylvia with her sandwich in one hand and a fold of her skirt in the other, which she pulled and twisted with tiny fingers.

Some of the geese turned their heads to stare at her. One or two backed away, but a couple of them noticed the bread in her hand. Sylvia saw the bread too. She stood up and looked down at the child. On her sandwich was a mixture of cheese and luncheon meat. She said, 'Birds like cheese. It's full of fat which is good for them.'

40

The girl gazed at Sylvia and gave a small laugh. She seemed too young to make conversation so Sylvia stood in silence for a few seconds and stared at the geese and the water. The girl let go of her skirt and tossed a piece of cheese from her sandwich on to the ground by her feet. It landed at least half a metre from the edge of the lake. One of the geese stretched out its neck to try to reach the cheese, but it was too far away. Sylvia frowned. 'If you're going to feed them, then place the cheese closer. They won't bite.'

The girl looked up. Her face seemed very tiny to Sylvia, and yet everything about it was adult, especially its expression, which was puffy and petulant. Even so, it was a child's face. She looked straight into Sylvia's eyes and said, 'Why should I?'

Sylvia paused and contemplated this question. 'Because you have to treat other animals with respect. If you don't, then they won't respect you.'

The girl moved forward slightly and pushed the cheese closer to the edge of the lake with her toe. As she did this, the pressure from her shoe covered the cheese with sand and dirt. Nevertheless, the goose reached for it again, stretching its neck thinly across the bank and opening its beak to try to grasp the cheese. But before it could do so, the little girl had lifted up one of her feet and had kicked at the gravel and dirt in front of her, blinding the goose with a spray of soil and stones.

It only took an instant. Before she knew what she was doing, Sylvia had grabbed hold of the girl and had thrown her, arms waving, legs kicking, into the lake. When it was done, she thought, Maybe she can't swim. What if the lake is deeper than it seems?

But it was too late. She was running.

She didn't turn back to look at the lake or the geese or the girl. She thought she heard screaming, but by then she was right by the park gates and on her way home. Not a scream, she decided, panting already, struggling to breathe. Not a scream, but the call of a crow.

EIGHT

Ruby unlocked the door and automatically reached out her hand for the light switch. She stopped herself just in time, feeling the switch with the tip of her finger but applying no pressure. Instead she paused in the doorway for a moment in order to adjust her eyesight to the room's darkness. After a few seconds she could make out the shape of a figure on the couch – Toro, still snoring – and she could also see, if she stood on tip-toe, beyond the sofa, where Vincent's blanket was bundled up into a deceptively large pile.

Very gently she closed the door behind her. She fancied a cup of coffee but didn't want to wake her guests, so she settled for a glass of water and then padded quietly into the bathroom.

It smelled. She closed the door and switched on the light. She was positive that the smell was of vomit, but could see no sign of it. She inspected the toilet bowl, which looked clean, but squirted some bleach down there for good measure.

After completing her ablutions, she switched off the bathroom light and made her way blindly into her bedroom. Before she closed the door she felt under the handle on both sides for the keyholes, located the key on the other side, took it out, pushed it in on her side, pulled the door to and locked it.

The small window in her bedroom let in just enough light. She pulled off her clothes and hunted around on the floor for something suitable to wear. Eventually she found a large T-shirt which she put on and pulled down.

She climbed into bed. Her blankets were rucked up and jumbled. She put out a hand to pull one over and then gasped as she touched something warm and bristly.

There lay Vincent in a state of irritable semi-wakefulness. He opened one eye and stared at her. 'Get your hands off my neck.'

She sprang out of bed. 'Christ! I locked myself in here and you're in here already.'

He pulled himself up on to his elbows, thought about saying something, opened his mouth to say it, but no words came out, only liquid.

Ruby was almost sick herself, but not in sympathy, not exactly.

'Get out of my bloody bed! You could be anybody!'

'I am anybody.'

He rolled over, stood up and staggered towards the door clutching his stomach. He pulled at the door handle with his free hand but it wouldn't open, so he threw up against it, then fell to his knees and inspected his handiwork.

'That's my kidney, liquidized.'

Ruby snatched a cardigan from the floor and wrapped it around her.

He groaned, 'You really think I intend taking advantage of you when I'm crippled by some kind of chronic gastric disorder?'

She pushed past him and switched on the light. They both blinked. Ruby's eyes adjusted. Vincent's wouldn't focus. He removed a hand from his gut long enough to touch his forehead and then clutched his stomach again, leaning forward. Ruby, fearing more mess, looked around for something he could vomit into, but didn't have a rubbish bin in the room or anything like a bowl or bag. Instead she grabbed hold of an old broken guitar without strings that was leaning against the wall. She thrust it towards him. 'Don't you dare be sick on the floor again.'

Vincent stared at the guitar. 'If you're expecting me to vomit into a musical instrument, I'd prefer a trumpet.'

He leaned even further forward and put a hand across his mouth, speaking through his fingers, 'Just open the door.'

She dumped the guitar, turned the key in the lock and pulled the door wide. He crawled through, and, after a moment's hesitation, dragged himself into the bathroom. Ruby glanced over at her bed and saw that his vomit was a particularly strange colour: a harsh taramasalata pink.

When Vincent crawled back out of the bathroom a short while later, he paused in the doorway and watched as Ruby stuffed all

43

affected linen into a refuse bag. She scowled at him. 'This pink stuff is like something you'd serve with crackers.'

She went and found a cloth in the kitchen and began to scrub at the door and the carpet. Vincent made no attempt to help her or to arrange himself comfortably. Instead he lay in a clumsy heap next to the wall.

She walked over to inspect him. He looked pale and sweaty. She prodded him with her toe.

'Are you asleep? The floor's rock hard.'

She touched his hand. It was wet.

She went into the living-room and leaned over the back of the sofa. 'Toro? Wake up.'

He grunted. 'You think I could sleep through that?'

She kicked at the back of the sofa. 'You got him pissed in the first place. Come and give me a hand.'

He sat up, rubbed his eyes. 'It smells like a hospital.'

She picked up the blanket from the floor and moved back towards the bedroom. 'Dettol. I cleaned everything.'

He followed her, lounged in the doorway and stared down at Vincent. 'Leave him. He's OK.'

She remade her bed. 'Lift him up. I've half a mind to call a doctor.'

Toro bent over and grabbed hold of Vincent's shoulders, then dragged him towards the bed, rucking up the carpet. They lifted him together and dumped him down on the blankets. He emitted a loud groan as his head hit the pillow. She arranged a couple of sheets over him, then perched on the edge of the bed and felt his forehead. Soaking. His lips were dry though. She peered up at Toro who was standing, looking bleary, feeling his own forehead.

'What's your game?' she said.

'What's the time?'

'Eleven-ish.' She looked down at Vincent. 'He couldn't throw up while he was asleep could he, and choke on it?'

Toro shrugged and went to find his coat. She heard the kitchen tap running, and then, a few seconds later, the front door closing. She looked down at Vincent. 'Fancy joining him?'

The room seemed very bright. She stood up, strolled into the living-room to check that the latch was down on the front door, then returned to the bedroom and switched off the light. The darkness soothed her eyes. She sat next to Vincent on the edge of her bed and stared at him. His eyes were flitting around under his eyelids. She said quietly, 'Are you dreaming? Do you want some tea? An ambulance?'

She yawned and looked over towards the window, bringing her legs up on to the bed and leaning her back against the headboard. The streets were still lively. Outside she could hear people talking and laughing. Inside everything was silent. She pulled one of the blankets over slightly so that it covered the top of her knees and thought, Isn't it strange how a place can be both noisy and quiet at the same time?

NINE

Samantha stayed out all Saturday night and returned to the flat shortly after midday on Sunday. The intervening time had been spent with her latest flame, Connor, who was tall, with a curtain of long brown hair that swung across his face, a slim body and smooth skin. They had known each other for several weeks. They had met at a charity benefit in Kentish Town. Connor had been performing with the main band, his own band, Stirsign. He was a drummer, and he sang too, in a scrappy, scraping, tuneless voice.

Sam had laughed at him from the side of the stage. She thought he looked ridiculous, smashing away at his drum-kit, bare-chested, his hair a mess, flying everywhere, his neck craning upwards towards an artfully placed microphone.

He spotted her immediately. She was the only girl there who found him funny. Girls didn't usually. When he'd introduced himself, later on, she'd said that she'd never come across a drummer who also sang. Connor had then proceeded to list every singing drummer he could think of. The way he saw it, the longer the list was, the longer she'd stay and talk.

'I just remembered, the drummer with Teenage Fanclub sings sometimes, and there was a band called Blyth Power a while ago whose drummer was the main vocalist, like me.'

Sam had smiled up at him, taking in every visible detail of his face through the silk-screen of her lashes. His voice was sexy, she decided, vaguely American, his tongue embracing a kind of cultured Southern twang. She appreciated the fact that he was self-assured. Confident men were the only kind she ever bothered with. Less brash, less aggressive men took one look and ran a mile.

She had been a late developer in the game of love. It was a game. Love was a diversion, but not an interest.

Men had never been at a premium in the Hackney flat. Her father, a Somalian student, a law student, had left home when she was three. In the long term she'd decided that this was a good thing. She had no silly expectations or preconceptions. She was beyond all that. Men couldn't disappoint her and they couldn't rule her.

Initially she had been too shy to push herself forward, preferring instead to think about things, to theorize and rationalize. But eventually she had learned to assert, if not herself, then a good approximation of herself – she always saved something, kept something back, which was the secret with men – and had learned how to flatter and to flirt. Love could be fun. You could get something out of it: sex or attention or ideas.

Connor had stared down at Sam's lips as he spoke to her, focusing on these instead of her eyes. 'What do you do? I don't want to bore you to death with talk of singing drummers all night.'

Sam smiled. 'I'm a singer too. A different kind of singer.'

An exotic singer, he thought, her hair drawn back, scraped back like a seal's. 'How different?'

'I sing in a band with my mother. We played the Bull and Gate last week.'

He grinned when she mentioned the venue, then said, 'I've never met anyone who played in a band with their mother before.'

'You have now.'

He asked her what kind of music they played but she didn't answer.

'It's more than that,' she said, finishing her drink. 'It's more complicated.'

'How?'

He liked her. But he only wanted small talk. That was his way. That was the whole point of flirting. He had a suspicion, though, that she was the kind of girl who didn't need to flirt.

She cleared her throat. 'Language is symbolic.' He flinched. She didn't notice. 'In other words, language represents things. And the way I see it, sexual representations work in the same way. I'll give you an example . . .'

He was watching her lips, not her eyes, watching how her teeth appeared and disappeared. Her teeth, the white crest of her mouth's pink wave. Rolling and rolling.

'Father and son. If I say that, it has positive associations. Hierarchy, order, calm, a kind of quiet power . . .'

He didn't care what she said. She was exquisite. He would agree and agree.

'But mother and daughter. I can say it, over and over, but it doesn't work as a symbol. It has no power.' She looked up at him. 'Are you following me?'

He nodded.

'Freud said daughters hate their mothers because all a daughter really wants is to have sex with her father. Mothers get in the way.'

Connor laughed. 'He really thought that?'

She nodded. 'But I'm not very interested in why symbols work the way they do, only in subverting them. I want to change them. I mean, there's such power between women. Mother and daughter. It should mean something. It does mean something, it just doesn't work at a symbolic level. And that's what I want to do, with the band. To help to create a new, positive, popular stereotype.'

As she spoke she saw Connor's face sag. She thought, I've blown my chances. He thinks I'm boring or strident or both.

When her lips stopped moving, Connor pushed his hair out of his eyes and asked, 'What does your mother think about all this?'

Sam grinned. 'She likes singing. She's always played the guitar. In fact she was in a girl group herself as a kid. She came over here from Dublin as a teenager in a band.'

He smiled at her. 'You're lucky. My mum has no fashion sense and she listens to Val Doonican.'

Sam laughed. 'Well, my mum wears Levis and she likes the Ronettes.'

Brera and Sam had always been close. Sam loved Brera because she was tolerant and quiescent and never pushy or judgemental. Brera loved Sam but often worried about her, even though she rarely articulated these worries. Instead she confided to Sam

48

her fears and concerns about Sylvia. Sylvia, her younger daughter, was, after all, her problem child. Sam had her flaws too, and Brera saw them, but she chose to hold her tongue.

In fact Brera thought Sam slept around too much. She couldn't understand her daughter's promiscuity. Sam had ideas about things which she was forever discussing. Brera acknowledged the ideas but ignored them. She thought, Sam needs to need a man. She just doesn't know it yet.

Sam and Connor arrived at the Hackney flat shortly after midday on Sunday. Although Brera sometimes found the situation with Sylvia difficult where strangers were concerned, Sam was entirely devoid of any sense of embarrassment. She had explained the situation fully to Connor shortly after their first night together. He had been confused but intrigued. He remained intrigued as Sam unlocked the door to the flat and invited him inside. The smell was pungent but tolerable. He'd had an aunt who kept chickens. It was comparable.

Brera was sitting on the living-room sofa watching *The Waltons*. She smiled up at them when they came in. 'Hi,' she said, 'I'll make you both something to eat when this finishes.'

Connor had been told that Brera was Irish, but, even so, was unprepared for her pinkness, her whiteness, the red of her hair. Sam was so different. And her sister? How many colours in one family? What did it mean? It had to mean something.

Sam linked her arm through Connor's and led him to her bedroom. She closed the door, pushed him up against it and put her arms around his neck. They kissed. She slid a hand under his T-shirt. He pulled away. 'The house seems so quiet.'

'You want some music on?'

Connor could hear someone coughing. He looked around the room, which was small but colourful. Above the bed was a large poster of the Judds. He walked over to it. 'I guess the Judds must be a big influence on you. The mother-and-daughter thing. The mother is really beautiful. They could be sisters.'

He sat down on Sam's bed. Sam took off her jumper and her shoes. She put them in a small wardrobe next to the door.

'I love the Judds, but sometimes I think they're a little bit too perfect, too polished.'

She bent down and pressed the play button on her tape recorder.

Connor frowned, failing to recognize the music. 'Who is this?'

Before Sam could answer, Brera had pushed open the door and had carried in a tray with two cups of tea and a plate of sandwiches. She said, 'It's Laverne Baker. Jackie Wilson's in the background. I hope you like garlic cheese.'

Connor was too surprised to respond. Sam looked unruffled. She put out her hands to take the tray.

Brera walked back towards the door. 'Steven phoned. He said he'd lined up a photographer for Tuesday.'

Sam offered Connor his mug of tea. 'That was quick.'

Brera nodded and closed the door behind her.

'Who's Steven?'

Sam picked up one of the sandwiches. 'Our new manager. We only met him yesterday.'

'You didn't tell me you were getting a manager.'

'Mum likes him. He's OK.'

Connor put down his mug and lay back on the bed. He stared up at the ceiling. She's so bloody secretive, he thought. Saves secrets like sweets. Eats them in private.

Sam moved to the end of the bed and pulled off his boots. He looked around the room again from his new vantage point and then held out his arms to her. 'Let's get this over with before your mother comes back in with lemonade and biscuits.'

Brera knocked on Sylvia's door and waited for her to answer. After a minute or so and a certain amount of scuffling and fluttering, Sylvia opened the door several inches and peered out.

'What?'

Brera offered her a mug of tea and a plate of sandwiches. Sylvia slid her hand through the crack and took the tea. 'I'm not hungry.'

'You should eat. I haven't even seen you since yesterday night when you went out. Where did you go?'

'Nowhere.'

Brera resisted the temptation to shove her foot into the crack in the door. Instead she said quickly, 'Sam's got her new friend around. Did you hear them come in?'

'No.'

'He's in a band too. They've been on television. He's called Connor. Sounds a bit American.'

Sylvia's face disappeared for a moment and then returned. 'I'll have a sandwich. Only one, though. Thanks.'

Her hand darted out and took a sandwich. Brera smiled. Sylvia nodded and then closed the door. Brera swallowed down her irritation. She went into the living-room, picked up her guitar and started to sing 'A Pair of Brown Eyes', strumming along in time.

Connor was mid-way through removing his trousers when he heard the conversation commence between Brera and Sylvia. He thought, I can't sustain an erection with those two chatting away like they're in the same room.

He pulled his trousers back on and did up the buttons. Sam groaned, exasperated, from her position on the bed and grabbed hold of her T-shirt. 'Why don't we go back to your flat? It was you who wanted to come here in the first place.'

Connor had half an ear on the conversation in the hallway. He turned down the music on the tape recorder and said, 'I didn't mean for us to come here for sex. I just wanted to meet everybody.'

He listened to their voices again. 'Your sister's voice is so hoarse. She sounds like Rod Stewart. Does she sing?'

Sam laughed. 'What do you think? She writes a weird kind of music. Like jazz but less tuneful. That's her contribution to things. She likes doing it. It's kind of methodical. She's hardly even got a speaking voice, though, let alone a singing one.'

As she spoke, Sam put on her T-shirt and picked up a book from her bedside table.

Connor moved a few steps closer to the door. He heard Brera mention his name.

Sam said tiredly, 'It's her allergy. If she tries to sing or shout her voice disappears altogether.'

'It sounds amazing, though, really distinctive.'

Sam looked up at him. 'The only reason she talks that way is because she's gradually choking herself. It's a slow process of strangulation.'

Connor felt foolish for being so enthusiastic. He turned towards her and changed the subject. 'What's that you're reading?'

She turned the page. 'Something about Hélène Cixous. She's this brilliant French intellectual. I've read all her stuff, but it's difficult. She's very controversial. She won't even call herself a feminist because feminism's too bourgeois.'

Connor looked down at the plate on the floor. 'What sort of cheese did your mother say this was?'

Sylvia sat on the end of her bed and drank her tea. The weather was turning. The day had started off warm and sticky. Now the sky was clouding over, was grey, heavy, lowering. The birds – at least a hundred or so – had flown inside as a consequence, in anticipation of the storm to come. They lined the walls of Sylvia's room, chattering and bickering. Several bounced to and fro across the carpet, scratching, preening and flapping their wings.

Sylvia thought, Above the bird noise I can hear Sam talking with that man. What are they discussing? What are they doing?

Sometimes she imagined what it would be like to have a male companion, but she couldn't really conceive of herself doing the things that normal women did. She couldn't imagine herself wanting the things that normal women wanted. She tried to feel pride in her abnormality, but she often felt as though her abnormality had become the only normal thing about her, the only relevant thing.

She sat on the end of her bed and drained the cup of its last few drops of tea. As she swallowed her tea, the incident in the park popped into her mind. The tea turned into dirty water in her mouth. She tried to swallow in air as the tea went down but she could not. She gagged on the liquid and it choked her. She imagined herself in the lake, with the mud and the slime and the tin cans. She imagined that she was the young girl and that she could not swim. She did not feel remorse, just fear. She wished that she could tie a tourniquet around her imagination, a piece of strong rope or cloth that could effectively cut off all dangerous ideas and fanciful notions, stop the flow of her thoughts from streaming, frothing, flooding and overwhelming her.

She could hear Brera singing in the living-room with her guitar. She tried to concentrate on this sound and to block out everything else. Then she heard Sam's voice. Sam had been laughing and talking before, but now she too had started to sing. Her voice toned in with Brera's perfectly. Brera sang in a higher register with a Celtic twang. Sam sounded very low and clear, like a soft, brown thrush – intense and lyrical.

She heard Sam emerge from her room and walk towards Brera's voice, still singing herself. She rolled her eyes towards the ceiling. They infuriated her. She found them unbearably smug and confident, like nuns or traffic wardens – self-assured and immensely self-motivated. Pure.

She inspected the eczema on her hands and wrists. The skin here was bumpy and itchy, some of it moist and shiny. She pulled off a scab which covered the tender flesh that linked the space between her finger and thumb. Her eyes watered. She enjoyed this strum of pain, lost herself in it and savoured its tone.

Suddenly she saw the little girl's face in the chafed and pinky pattern of her flesh, imagined for a second how the cold water would have felt entering her nose and throat, covering her eyes.

The sound of Connor's hesitant tread in the hallway distracted her. She stopped breathing for a moment and listened out for the slight noises he made, her head to one side, eyes closed. He had a light tread. Must be thin, she thought. His step seemed tentative, well-meaning, self-conscious. She heard him enter the living-room and began breathing again. The air she drew into her lungs felt dry and coarse. It rattled in her throat. She coughed for a short while then swallowed down a mouthful of phlegm.

Connor was singing now too. He was doing a comic version of

Dolly Parton's 'Love is like a Butterfly', in a low, brash voice. She could hear the two women laughing. She put her hands over her ears, imagined that her hands were like shells, and the noise of the blood, the compressed air in her ears, the wail in her head, was really the sea. She stood on a bone-pale beach. It was an airless place.

TEN

Ruby awoke to the sound of the telephone ringing. She opened her eyes and tried to pull herself up straight. She'd been slumped over sideways on to her bedside table. Her face felt strange, like warm wax that had set overnight into a distorted, lopsided shape. Her neck ached, even her tongue ached and her body felt, in its entirety, distinctly askew.

Vincent was there. Ugh! She looked at him. A horrible face. Dirty. Phlegm, mucus, special smells. Blood, dried. Everything inside spilling out.

His face was a solid bruise. He was a car accident, still jumbled. She had no clear impression of him. Not mentally, not visually. It was bright in her room, a yellow-white brightness, reflecting unkindly off him.

She sprang out of bed to answer the ringing. She was still wearing her cardigan, which she pulled close around her, and her T-shirt, which she noticed had coffee stains down the front.

The telephone – it had a long extension cord – was situated in the centre of the draining-board next to the sink. She picked up the receiver. 'Yeah? Ruby here.'

She licked a finger and applied it, somewhat hopelessly, to the stain.

'You sound rough.'

She didn't recognize the voice. 'Hold on.'

She put down the receiver, turned on the cold tap and stuck her head under it, inhaling sharply as the water gushed over her hair, into her ears and down her neck. She turned it off and shook her head, like a dog after a dip, then picked up the receiver again. 'Hi.'

She felt the water dripping down her back and her face. Eventually a voice said, 'Hello, Ruby?'

'Yeah.'

'Donald Sheldon. Is it too early?'

'I've been up ages,' she lied. He'd never phoned her before.

He said, 'Actually, I'd like to see you. This afternoon if it's possible.'

'Oh. OK.'

'There's a café near Seven Sisters tube.' He described its precise location. 'We could meet twelve-ish.'

Twelve was too early.

'Yeah, that's fine. Seven Sisters. Twelve-ish.'

'See you then.'

She put down the receiver and walked into the bathroom to look for a towel. She found one slung over the edge of the bath and wrapped up her dripping hair in it before putting the plug in the bath and turning on the taps.

Back in her bedroom, she rooted out a pair of jeans, a black vest and some clean underwear. Vincent lay across the bed, his legs spread, his feet dangling off the end. His arms, she noticed, now held a pillow over his face. She said, 'I wouldn't do that. Someone might be tempted to press down on it.'

He said nothing.

She returned to the bathroom. While she undressed, she debated how soon it would be acceptable to ask him to leave. She tested the water with her hand, climbed in, then lay back and relaxed, staring abstractly beyond her breasts, her knees, her toes, at the taps and the steam from the water.

Vincent felt like a caterpillar changing into a butterfly. That inbetween stage. A pupa. His skin, hard, semi-impervious; himself, inside, withered and formless.

He was not himself. His head bumped and pumped. The light, the morning, scorched him.

During the night he had awoken, he didn't know what time, and had found a girl, a stranger, next to him. Her hip near his chin. Wool, scratching; cold skin. He had pressed his forehead against her thigh. It had cooled him.

And now it was morning. He needed something. Had

56

to stretch his body – that crumpled thing – his mind, his tongue.

Ruby picked up a bar of soap and started to build up a lather. What does Sheldon want? she wondered. What does he want from me? Her toes curled at the prospect. She stared at them and thought, Why am I doing that with my feet?

Vincent stood on the other side of the bathroom door with his hand on the handle. He shouted, 'You could've told me you were having a bath.'

Ruby dropped the soap and covered her breasts. 'Don't you dare come in.'

'I have no intention of coming in,' he said scathingly. After a pause he added, 'Why the hell did you bring me here? I've had the worst time.'

She gasped at this, her expression a picture, and shouted, 'I didn't bring you here.'

'Well, I didn't get here on my own.'

His voice sounded muffled, further away now. 'Do you always live like this?'

She stood up, indignant, and stepped out of the bath. 'Like what?'

Silence, then, 'Forget it.'

'Like what?'

She grabbed a towel, wrapped it around her and pulled open the door. 'Live like what?'

He was standing in the kitchen, looking inside one of her cupboards. He glanced at her, in the towel. 'For a minute there,' he said, grinning, 'I thought you were a natural blonde. But it's only foam.'

She yanked the towel straight. With his cut, his pale, white face, the bruises, the suggestion of a black eye, he looked like Frankenstein's monster. But he didn't frighten her. She said calmly, 'Get out of my flat.'

He grimaced. 'Some hospitality. I have a migraine and all you can do is shout.'

'Yeah?' She smiled. 'Well, I think you should go.'

She returned to the bathroom, closed the door, dropped her towel.

He said, 'I have a blotch. I'm going blind. You expect me to go when I can't even see straight?'

She stared at the bath. 'Well, whose fault is that?'

She picked up her towel and started to dry herself. She heard the cupboard close.

'Yours. You shouldn't have paid my bail.'

She rubbed herself vigorously.

'And lunch. I only get migraines from gherkins.'

'What?'

'An allergy.'

She laughed. She was glad that he had an allergy.

He listened to her laughing. Smiled at it. He liked her flat. It was central. He sat down on the sofa, picked up one of the empty vodka bottles, sniffed the neck of it and winced.

Eventually she emerged, fully dressed, made up, her teeth brushed and her hair gelled.

'I made you some tea.' He held out a mug to her.

She took it from him. 'Aren't you having any?'

He shook his head. 'Couldn't keep it down.'

'Did you try?'

'I had some water.'

She sipped the tea. It was luke-warm. 'How are you feeling?'

He shrugged.

'What are you going to do?'

He shrugged again.

'Will you go home? Are you up to it?'

He cleared his throat. 'May I use your bathroom?'

'Of course you can.'

Once he'd closed the door she shouted, 'I'm going out in a minute. Should I trust you here alone?'

'I wouldn't.'

She put down her mug of tea. 'Only a trustworthy person would've said that.'

'Think what you like.'

'I will.'

58

She picked up her keys. She was insured. She needed a new stereo, anyway.

Donald Sheldon – self-appointed king of Hackney Wick – was a short, squat man with thick, wavy hair and skin the colour of roasted peanuts. He was drinking a foamy coffee and wore an expensive business suit. Ruby was nervous, had thought too much about meeting him.

'Am I late?'

He shrugged. 'Ten minutes. Coffee?'

She nodded. 'Thanks.'

He manœuvred himself out from behind the table and strolled over to the counter. Ruby watched him. She regularly saw him down at the track. He trained mainly at Hackney, but she was well informed that he ran his dogs wherever he could. She'd often seen him interviewed on SIS, the racing channel.

He returned to the table, carrying her coffee, holding on to its saucer. She looked down at his hands and saw that he wore rings on most fingers but none that seemed like a wedding ring. He sat down again. 'I've seen you at Hackney a lot. You obviously enjoy the sport.'

She nodded.

'How old do you think I am?'

This question surprised her. She stared at his face, his thick hair, his good tan. She wanted to flatter him. 'Forty, forty-two.'

He smiled. 'Forty-eight. I've been racing dogs since I was fourteen.'

'Thirty-four years.'

'I first went to Hackney when I was five, with my dad. You might get to meet him later.'

She stared at him, bemused, wondering where his dad fitted into the equation.

He smiled fondly, but more to himself than at her. 'My dad got me my first dog. He helped pay for it by putting his every last penny on Pigalle Wonder in the 1958 London Cup. A great champion: big, but well balanced. Really handsome.'

Ruby put her teaspoon in her coffee and stirred away some of the foam. She felt obliged to say something but couldn't think what, so she just said, 'Betting on the dogs is a bit of a lottery.'

Don looked irritated. 'I tell you, the only important thing you need to do to win at the dogs, Ruby, is to rely on honest thinking.'

She liked the way he'd used her name. She looked into his face. Did he want to employ her or to fuck her? Either way, she was flattered. He was saying, 'Racing isn't just about speed.'

He paused. 'Do you know what it is that makes a good dog?'

Ruby focused on her coffee and tried to think. Eventually she said, 'Speed and intelligence, mainly.'

He shook his head. 'Racing is all about negotiating bends. To negotiate a bend you need balance, coordination and muscular control. But it's more than that. A dog must have the will to win. It has to have that primitive urge. Some dogs will always be chasers or chuckers. A dog must know how to place itself. It's got to be crafty.'

She looked at his hands as he spoke. Brown, clean hands. What did he want? What was he doing?

He said, 'I didn't know anything when I got my first dog.'

An image shot into her mind of how Donald Sheldon would look naked. She visualized him with an all-over tan and pinky-brown genitals. Not too much body hair. His stomach, slightly saggy, and his breasts.

He said, 'All this is leading somewhere.'

'Is it?'

Of course. He looked at her, grinned, then said, 'And I think I have a good idea where you want it to lead.'

His voice sounded suggestive, arrogant, even sensual. He was old. Not that old. She inhaled deeply and stared straight into his eyes. He picked up a fork and shook it for emphasis, 'I'm willing to sell you that dog.'

'Dog?'

'The one we discussed.'

'Discussed?' Ruby wanted to rewind this conversation in order to try to make sense of it.

He dropped the fork, laced his fingers together and leaned

forward. 'She's trained. She's in good form. I mean, she's out of season now and she's in good nick. She's registered. She has a race or two lined up at Hackney, but after that it'd be your business.'

He was trying to sell her something! Donald Sheldon!

I would never, she thought, holding in her gut, I would never have had sex with him. Never.

He added, 'It must be about her fourteenth week since she was in season. She's probably got a bit rusty while she was rested, but that's only natural.'

Ruby tried desperately to remember what she had said to him, how this situation had developed. Had he confused her with someone else? I didn't even want a job, she thought furiously. Not that kind of job.

He frowned. 'She's put on weight, but bitches often do, even if they haven't been mated. Her current grading figure isn't very encouraging, but I'd be giving her to you for nine hundred.'

She said carefully, 'To be honest, cash-flow is a bit of a problem for me at the moment.'

She wanted to laugh in his face. It was all so stupid.

He shrugged. 'I wouldn't want the money straight off. A week would do. Six days. If we shook on it now you could take her immediately.'

He was squinting with sincerity. He sincerely thought he was doing her a favour. If he'd employed her, if he'd fucked her, he would've worn that same expression. But he was selling her something.

Selling her something.

She had to admire him.

He waited.

It was her turn. To do. What?

She took the easiest option, as was her nature.

She nodded and shook his hand. His skin was warm and dry.

He stood up. 'The dog's down at the kennels. Here . . .' He handed her his card, which she took and inspected.

'My dad'll be there for most of the afternoon. He's expecting you.'

'Thanks.'

'I'm not doing you any favours. I've had very little luck with this particular bitch. But you expressed an interest and now she's yours.'

Ruby tried to smile as she placed his card in the front pocket of her jeans. He turned to go. She watched him as he walked between the tables and up to the door. He pushed it, it swung outwards and he stepped outside.

She raised her eyes to the ceiling and noticed a large fan up there, turning rapidly.

Which particular bitch? When had she spoken to him at the track? Had he been holding a dog at the time? Had she been holding one? Had she expressed an interest?

She felt hot. The fan's rapid movements were making her feel queasy. She pulled off her jacket and walked outside. It was hot here too. Things were fuzzy. She blinked, unable to tell whether this fuzziness was caused by heat, a heat-wave shimmering on the Sunday roads, or by movements behind her eyes, inside her.

Vincent pottered around the flat, feeling no particular urge to leave. He tried to assess Ruby on the basis of her personal possessions, but there was little of interest to look at apart from her record collection and her underwear. The record collection was impressive.

His headache was now a dumb whine at the back of his skull, but tolerable. He found an old Kraftwerk album and put it on – turning down the volume slightly – then wandered about, acclimatizing, inspecting things.

He had a bath. It felt like ages since he'd had a proper wash. He picked up Ruby's soap and sniffed it. It wasn't strongly perfumed – smelled like Palmolive – so he used it freely, grinning to himself, imagining which parts of Ruby's body it had lathered. The warmth of the water, the rubbing, the foam, gave him a slight erection. He stared at it for a while with a terse and serious expression, then burst out laughing. It bobbed down in the water, submissive again, mournful and flaccid.

After drying himself, he went into the kitchen, still naked, did the washing up and then returned to the bathroom, where he picked up his clothes, dressed and surveyed himself in the mirror. His whole forehead was a pinky-purple colour. This bruising reached down to either side of his eyes. One eye was black. He inspected the cut more thoroughly. Most of the bump had gone down, but several strands of hair were caught inside the mouth of the gash. He pulled at them, very gently, wincing as some of them came out. He pulled a few more and then gave up, concerned that he might bring back his headache.

He returned to the kitchen and inspected the cupboards to see what food Ruby had in. Tinned stuff, dried stuff. He'd cook something.

While some beans were soaking he tidied up the living-room and then moved into Ruby's bedroom. Her carpet was knee-deep in pieces of clothing. He kicked these into a large pile and then sorted out what was clean and what was dirty. He sniffed, looked, fondled.

He liked it here. He'd stay for a while, but he wouldn't ask. If you asked, people said no. Even soft people. Eventually.

Ruby pressed the buzzer and listened out for barking, but could hear none. The building was a mixture of grandeur and delapidation. It was built in a square around a tarmacked courtyard. The entrance was barred by a large, black, metal gate.

After several minutes a tiny old man staggered across the courtyard towards her. He looked like Mr Punch, all nose and chin with eyes like sultanas. He reached the gate, puffed out, and gazed through it at her. 'You've come to get the bitch?'

Ruby nodded and said, 'I've seen you at Hackney before, haven't I?'

'Could've, but I'm usually at Walthamstow.'

He started to unlock the gate before adding, 'That bitch of yours wouldn't run on the Walthamstow track for love nor bloody money. They've got a McGee hare there. You familiar with it?'

Ruby frowned. 'It's smaller, isn't it?'

'Smaller than the Outside Sumner and doesn't make so much

63

noise. Stupid bitch wouldn't run for it. Trap opened and she didn't come out. Nice grass track but she wouldn't have any of it.' He shook his head. 'Racing manager was about ready to kill me. Punters weren't happy either. There again, she was still a novice, so she probably only had about fifty quid on her.'

He pulled the gate open. Ruby stepped inside and he closed it behind her, then turned and led the way across the tarmac. She followed him, watching the back of his yellowy kennel coat, into the main building, through an unprepossessing passageway, which smelled of detergent and dog, and into a large, square, brightly lit kitchen.

He pointed towards the big pine table that filled the centre of the room. 'Sit down while I go get her. I'll bring her registration booklet too.'

Ruby sat down and rested her elbows on the table. The room felt airless, she felt aimless. Why was she here? She thought, I won't think anything. Not anything. Nothing.

When he returned, she said, 'Don didn't get around to telling me your name.'

He grinned. False teeth. As straight as a die. 'Stanley. Stan. I'm seventy-four and he still has me working a seven-day week.'

Ruby pushed herself back on her chair and peered over at the dog. Stan was holding a lead and the bitch stood at the end of it, looking tense. She couldn't help thinking how large the animal seemed. Not fat, just big.

Stan leaned against the table and got his breath back. The dog stood still, not pulling on her leash, but managing to look on edge, padding from foot to foot. He stared down at her. 'I like black bitches. This one's related to Dolores Rocket. Won the Derby. Won the Puppy Oaks too, twenty-odd years ago.'

He jerked the lead and brought the dog's head up. Her face was skinny, scraggy and strangely petulant.

'I'll get a muzzle on her.'

'Do you have to?'

'She'll chase anything if she feels the urge.'

'Anything but the McGee hare, eh?'

Stan fitted the muzzle over the dog's face. 'Well, they've all got

64

coursing in their blood, but these dogs . . .' He slapped her lightly on her rump and she stiffened her legs to take the slap. 'These dogs were bred from strains of dogs that didn't so much care what they chased, they'd run for anything.'

He brought the bitch around the table and handed Ruby her lead. Ruby hesitated and then took it. She felt a dart of terror in her chest that started between her breasts and shot up to her throat. She tried to swallow it, to keep it under.

Stan looked down at her for a moment, then said conspiratorially, 'How much is he asking for?'

Ruby felt the leather of the lead between her finger and her thumb. 'Nine hundred.' When she said it, it meant nothing.

He burst out laughing. 'I'll tell him you'll give him seven. He had her down at Swaffham in Norfolk on Friday. Check her toes.'

Ruby picked up the dog's right foot. The pads all seemed fine. She picked up the left and he interrupted her, taking hold of the paw himself and parting the front pads. 'Third pad's slightly swollen.'

'Is that a problem?'

She knew it was. I know all this, she thought, I know this stuff.

'I'll tell Don you thought it was.'

She smiled gratefully and stroked the dog's back. 'How did she do at Swaffham? I didn't even know Don raced in that part of the country.'

'How do you think she did?'

He passed Ruby the registration booklet. She opened it. *Little Buttercup. Black bitch* . . . When she was born, where, the names of her parents, the size of the litter. Physical description. Tiny details. Times of her races, places. *Swaffham* – the latest entry.

'Sixth.'

'She's got a race lined up at Hackney on Thursday. You'd better have a chat with the racing manager, though. He's not happy with this bitch. Did Don tell you she's in the E grade? Her actual running time at 525 yards was 30.40 on her last night out.'

Ruby verified this in the booklet. It wasn't a good time.

'Just the same,' he added, noting her expression, 'there's

nothing wrong with her physically. The toe's no problem. You've obviously got a good eye. She's a fine-looking bitch.'

Suddenly, at last, she remembered. A month ago, Hackney Wick, the traps were loaded. Six dogs. The hare, starting, the squeal of it. Some dogs, barking, whining. And then. She remembered it. Her trap. Number six. A tail, sticking out through the bars at the front.

'She turned around!' Ruby said. 'In the trap. She turned around in the trap, and I thought . . .' Ruby had thought, That's only logical. She turned around because that's the direction the hare's coming from. And Don was furious. He said . . . and I said . . . and he said . . . and I said, 'But she's a fine-looking bitch.'

Stan was staring at her, nervously.

'Sorry,' she said, almost laughing with relief, 'I just thought of something.'

'Don didn't say what you were planning to do with her.'

'I don't know. He said she had a couple of races lined up.'

'One race on Thursday.'

Ruby was thinking now, planning. 'I'd better get a licence.'

He stared at her blankly. 'She's not your only dog?'

'My first.' She liked this idea. She'd been sloppy, before, admittedly.

'Have you got kennels?'

'No.' She said this with great certainty, as though only saying it this way would mean it didn't matter.

'You won't get a licence then. Not without proper kennels. Anyway, when the racing manager at Hackney finds out Don isn't training her any more, he'll drop her from the card. If she doesn't get a place in her next race, he'll drop her for the season anyway.'

Ruby stared at the dog. The dog's expression was docile but furtive.

'You,' she said, with sudden fondness.

The dog licked her lips. Her whiskers stuck out of her cheeks – silver against her black fur – like needles in a pincushion.

After a while Ruby said, 'There's no law against being too keen.'

'There should be, though.'

Stan leaned against the table. 'You could run her at an independent track and you wouldn't even need a licence. Swaffham's a permit track. You could run her there for fifty quid. Or you could even breed from her.'

'I could,' she said. 'I could, but I don't want to.' She was making decisions now. She could make them. 'I want to run her at Hackney.'

'You can't.'

'I can run her on Thursday.'

'He'll drop her if he finds out Don's sold her.'

'What if she got a place?'

He laughed. 'She won't.'

'But what if she did?'

'He'll drop her anyway.'

'She deserves a chance.'

Stan thought about this, looked unconvinced, but said, 'If I come down on the day, and anyone asks, you can say you're with me.'

Ruby smiled. 'I've got plans for her.'

Stan stuck his hands deep into his pockets. 'You'll find out soon enough she's got plans of her own.'

Vincent scowled at the dog. 'Where did that come from?'

Ruby closed the door behind her and unclipped Buttercup's lead from her collar.

'She's a bitch. I just bought her.'

'Why?'

She sat down. 'I don't know.'

He stared at the dog as she walked around the room, sniffing furniture and poking her nose into corners.

'Black's a good colour. She matches everything,' he said.

'Yeah. I really needed to hear that.'

'I made dinner.'

'I thought you'd be gone.'

'Sorry to disappoint you.'

He went into the kitchen and dished up the food he'd prepared.

'Don't give any to the dog.'

'I wasn't planning to.'

'She's on a diet.'

Ruby took the plate he handed her and started eating. Tuna, rice, sweetcorn, beans. The dog smelled the food and walked over. She sat next to Ruby, staring at the plate, her tail making a slight swishing sound against the carpet.

'Does she bite?'

'I don't think so.'

'Why's she wearing that muzzle?'

Ruby closed her eyes, stopped chewing and swallowed. 'At Tottenham Court Road tube she chased a woman wearing a fur-trimmed jacket up the escalator.'

He laughed. 'Did she get her?'

'She caught her but she didn't bite her. She was wearing her muzzle.'

'You should've had her on a lead.'

Ruby dropped her fork and showed him her hand. 'Leather burns.'

She continued eating. 'This is nice.'

'I trained as a chef. In Dublin. They had a big dog track there. Shelbourne Park. I went once but I never won a penny.'

'There are always plenty of jobs for chefs up west. Imagine what you could earn. You could pay me back in no time.'

'I don't think so.'

He stood up and went to turn over the record he'd been listening to earlier, then ran some water into a pan and put it down on the floor for the dog.

'Can she drink through that muzzle?'

'Yeah.'

He returned to the sofa, noting Ruby's miserable expression. 'I get the feeling you didn't really think this through.'

'Story of my life.'

She continued eating, then added, 'But there was a great moment back then when it really did seem like a good idea.'

'She'll chew this flat to pieces.'

'I'll keep her muzzled.'

'What will you do with her when you're at work?'

The dog, suddenly, inexplicably, started to bark. Vincent jumped and dropped a forkful of rice on to his lap. He scooped it up with his fingers and crammed it into his mouth. Ruby craned her neck and stared over the back of the sofa towards Buttercup, who was still standing next to her bowl of water.

'What's up?'

She called out her name but the dog didn't respond, so she put down her plate and walked over to her, squatted down next to her and tried to attract her attention. The dog continued to bark, loudly, bouncing forward on her front paws. Ruby tried to force her to sit by pushing down her rump but the dog wouldn't oblige. She tried talking sternly and then, finally, shouting.

Vincent put down his plate and walked over. 'What's she barking at?'

'I don't know. She was fine when she came in.'

The dog fell silent. They both stared at her, surprised. Then, after a five-second hiatus, she started up again.

Ruby swore.

'If the bloody neighbours find out I've got a dog, I'll be evicted.'

'Follow her eyes.'

'Why?'

She peered into Buttercup's face. The dog's eyes were glazed and purposeful. Her breath was bad.

Vincent bounded over to the stereo and lifted the stylus. The dog stopped barking. He dropped it again. She barked.

'She doesn't like Kraftwerk, so she's barking at the speakers.'

He squatted down, took the record off and threw it on the floor, then put another one on.

Ruby's eyes widened. 'Be careful. You'll scratch them.'

He turned the volume up and waited for a song to start. As soon as it did, so did the dog. He laughed and switched it off. 'She doesn't like Inner City either.'

He took out a Ray Charles album and slung it on. It began to play. The dog cocked her head, listened intently and then sat down.

'Look at her! She's an old crooner.'

He was preparing to change the record yet again when Ruby crawled over to the socket in the wall and pulled out the plug. She glared at him, still on her hands and knees. 'If you've scratched any of my records you can pay me for them.'

'I won't scratch them.'

'I bet you already have.'

He picked up one and inspected the vinyl. Ruby squatted down next to the dog and stroked her. She said, 'She's all upset. Her heart's beating like crazy.' After a few seconds she added, 'You can tell everything you need to know about a dog's condition when you stroke it. She's got strong, wide shoulders, a good, firm back . . .'

I'll get him to stay, she thought, at least for tomorrow. He can look after her while I'm out, until she gets used to this place. He can take her to Hyde Park.

She continued to stroke the dog, who rested her chin on the carpet and closed her eyes.

Vincent watched this. He realized something. They wouldn't get around to sex now. That's what the dog meant. He hadn't really considered sex, planned it, wanted it. Even so.

He snapped the record he was holding in half. It was a sharp, clean break. They both stared at him: Ruby, the dog.

'You're going to replace that record.'

He smiled. Of course he would. He studied the two halves to see what it was.

Ruby picked up the dog's lead and attached it to her collar.

'Where are you going? You haven't finished eating yet.'

She ignored him, pulled on her jacket, checked for her keys and then opened the door. He was a bastard. She wanted to punch him. She stepped out into the hallway, the dog at her heels.

He stood up. 'If anywhere's open,' he shouted after her, 'You're completely out of milk.'

70

There was a painting in the living-room, a portrait, that Connor especially hated. 'That's her,' he said, when he first showed Sam around his flat, 'Sarah. I share this place with her.'

Sam liked the painting. It was creepy. A female nude. Lips, russet nipples, ribs.

'Does she really look like that?'

He laughed. 'She thinks she does. She's so vain. You'll meet her.'

'Where is she?'

'Los Angeles for a month. Helping to research a book on the paranormal.'

Sam was fascinated. 'Para-normal. Not normal.'

'She's a researcher.'

'And you don't like her?'

The flat, she could tell, was the site, the centre, of subtle guerilla warfare. A picture; a wall-hanging; garish, orange hessian curtains. All Sarah's contributions. Sam grew accustomed to spotting her in objects. Teapots, candles, cosmetics in the bathroom.

Connor claimed to be an aesthete. He said he hated clutter. But his bedroom, his territory, was full of musical flotsam: a drum-kit, African bongos, symbols, a tambourine. His records, his stereo.

Sam couldn't learn much here, though. In the living-room, she inspected the bookshelves.

'Henry James?'

'Hers.'

'Kurt Vonnegut?'

'Mine.'

'*Psychoanalysis: the Impossible Profession*?'

'Hers.'

'*Dead Babies*?'

'Mine.'

'*Skinhead Escapes*?'

'Mine.'

She picked this book up. It was a cheap, trashy novella. She didn't like it. She found it distasteful. 'I wouldn't want to own something like this.'

'It'll probably be worth a fair bit in a few years' time.'

'It's exploitative.'

He nodded. 'But sometimes that kind of stuff can be interesting.'

'Oh.'

She put the book back on the shelf.

Connor. He was interested in everything. She'd learned this very quickly. He was pragmatic. And what was she? Idealistic. Full of ideals.

Connor's problem, the way she saw it, was that he was interested in too much. He was funny and gentle, but he was fascinated by stupid, sometimes even bad, things.

'My parents,' Connor explained, 'rented this place to Sarah while I was at college. She's always been here.'

Sam liked her. I've been living with this woman, she thought, learning all about her.

It was early morning. Connor was still asleep. She'd risen to get herself a drink of water. On her way back to bed she paused in front of the painting. Bones, white flesh, red hair, red eyes. It was hung on the wall adjacent to Sarah's room. Connor, she thought, is still sleeping. She touched the door handle, shuddered, pressed it down. Pushed.

Inside, the curtains were drawn. The bedspread was patchwork. She could smell patchouli oil. On the dressing-table, however, she noticed bottles of what appeared to be more sophisticated scent. She walked over and picked up a bottle of Rive Gauche, tentatively sprayed it into the air and sniffed. Next to the bed – she sat down and inspected it – was a book of women's erotica. She opened it. Marilyn French. Anaïs Nin. She

72

started to read, struggling in the half-light to focus on its ant-black print.

'Hello.'

Samantha gave a start, almost dropping the book and the perfume. A tall, very thin woman stood in the doorway, grinning sardonically. She had bright, hennaed hair and a gaunt, striking face. In her hand she held a suitcase.

'What are you reading?'

'You must be Sarah.'

Sam stood up and quickly put the perfume back down on the dresser. 'I shouldn't be in here.'

Sarah walked into the room, threw her suitcase down on the bed, strolled over to the window and drew the curtains.

'What were you reading?'

'Angela Carter.'

'Were you enjoying it?'

Sam nodded.

'You must be Connor's new friend.'

Sam didn't much like this description of herself, but nodded again.

Sarah stared at her. Sam wore only a dressing-gown with nothing underneath. She tightened the belt self-consciously.

'That picture,' she said, confused and embarrassed, 'in the living-room. It does look just like you.'

Sarah laughed at this. 'Connor's been telling you about my monumental ego.'

'No. I didn't mean that.'

'The print is by Schiele. He's very famous. He painted male nudes too.'

She opened her suitcase and peered at its jumbled contents.

'How was Los Angeles?'

'OK. I was working. Do you work?'

'I'm a singer.'

'Not with Connor's group?'

'No. I'm in a band with my mother.'

'That's a novelty.'

73

She started to unpack. 'I'd rather strangle my mother than sing with her.'

Sam closed the book she was holding and put it down on the dressing-table.

'You can borrow that if you like.'

'Thanks.' She picked it up again.

'Angela Carter,' Sarah said, frowning. 'You like her?'

Sam nodded.

'The way I see it,' Sarah said, pulling out some clothes and shoving them into a wicker washing-basket at the foot of her bed, 'there are two types of women. Those who think we're the same as men, and those who think we're different. Equal, obviously, but different.'

Sam was delighted. A proper conversation! Connor's idea of animated chat was a discussion of the intricacies of Gram Parson's fretwork.

'Which type are you?' she asked.

'The first. But I don't know about Angela Carter, and that makes me suspicious.'

'I like her,' Sam said, 'I like that difference. Whatever it is.'

Sarah considered this for a moment and then said, 'Maybe because you're culturally different, you have a looser approach to questions of gender.'

'Culture doesn't come into it,' Sam said, vaguely defensive. 'I might be a different colour, but I still know that sex is more complicated than race.'

Sarah continued to unpack. She took some magazines from her case, some papers and a notepad.

'Connor,' she said, smiling, 'must find you a challenge.'

'How?'

'Politically.'

Sam tried to understand this. 'It's not politics I'm interested in. It's something more subtle.'

'Subtle?' She laughed. 'You think Connor's up to that?'

Sam stared at her. How could she respond?

Connor appeared in the doorway and saved her. 'Hello,' he said, nodding at Sarah. 'So you got back in one piece?'

74

'I landed at five.'

He turned to Sam. 'I wondered where you'd got to.'

He hitched up the sheet he was holding around his hips.

Sam moved towards the door. 'I suppose I'd better leave you to it.'

Sarah nodded. 'But keep the book as long as you like.'

Sam thanked her, tucking the book under her arm.

Back in his room, Connor yanked off the sheet and climbed into bed. 'I heard what she was saying. She'd have eaten you alive.'

'I don't think so.'

'No?'

'But I felt really stupid.'

'That's ridiculous.'

Sam paused for a moment and then said, 'Why don't you like her?'

He puffed up his pillow. 'I wouldn't mind her if I didn't have to live with her.'

'She's abrasive.'

'Yeah.'

'Threatening.'

'What?'

'Maybe because she's clever.'

'Opinionated.'

'Because she's a feminist.'

He rubbed his face with his hands. 'So are you.'

'You just don't like aggressive women.'

'That's stupid.'

'If she was a man, you wouldn't mind her.'

'I don't like aggressive men either.'

He turned over, on to his side, making room for her in the bed. She hadn't yet decided whether she wanted to join him when the doorbell rang. He sat up. 'We're rehearsing this morning.'

'But what about Sarah?'

He frowned. 'What about her?'

'She's been awake half the night. You can't practise now.'

He smiled. 'Can't I?'

'Bastard.'

He stood up. Unexpectedly, the sight of his thin, naked body aroused her. She put out her hand and touched his back. He turned, smiled, moved closer. She whispered, 'Let's have sex.'

Outside she could hear Sarah answering the door, sounds in the living-room, male voices.

He stroked her hair. 'No rubbers. You wouldn't want me to re-use one.'

He bent over to pick up some shorts. She hit him across his rump with a tambourine and said tartly, 'You don't need a condom to give head.'

As she reached consciousness, Brera rolled over and focused dozily on her alarm clock. Nine-thirty. It was Monday. She signed on every Monday. Every Monday at nine. She sat up. She was late. Something was wrong. Something was missing. Suddenly she knew. Sylvia! Sylvia always wakes me!

She sprang out of bed, then froze, barely breathing, listening intently. At first she could hear nothing. Then she heard a noise, the faintest of sounds: a desperate, rattling, guttural wheezing.

She sprinted into the hallway. Sylvia's bedroom door was closed. She didn't knock, she flew in. Sylvia was on the floor, clutching her throat, in her own stranglehold, tossing and turning.

The room was full of birds. When Brera ran in they left their perches and filled the air – there must have been sixty of them – aiming upwards, towards the ceiling, in a feathery whirlwind. She found them terrifying, but she kept her wits, fell to her knees and grabbed hold of Sylvia, whose face was a whitey-purple colour, her lips flecked with foam. She took hold of her shoulders, slid her hands firmly under her armpits and dragged her out.

She lay her down flat, in the hallway, and dashed back into the bedroom. She searched around on the floor for a few seconds, then looked on the bed and finally found what she was hunting for on top of Sylvia's grey trunk: her inhaler. She snatched hold of it, kept her head low (the birds were still flying, calling, panicking) and ran out, slamming the door behind her.

Sylvia had begun to jerk and convulse. Brera pushed the inhaler between her lips. 'Exhale and then breathe this in. Exhale!'

Sylvia turned her face away. Brera jammed Sylvia's head between her knees and forced the inhaler into her mouth again, even deeper this time. She pressed it, and it pumped its fumes into her.

'Breathe it in! Breathe it in, you stupid thing!'

The inhaler had little or no effect. Brera began to panic.

'Sam? Where is she?'

She closed her eyes for a moment and tried to think what Sam would do, then pulled Sylvia along the hallway and into the living-room. This was an airy room. She dragged her towards the door that led out on to the roof, wrenched the door open. 'It's fresh air. Breathe it in. Go on!'

Sylvia's body was shuddering and gyrating. Brera hauled her on to the roof, out into the open air. She felt the cold tarmac on her bare feet and knees. She opened Sylvia's lips, inhaled deeply herself and then attempted mouth to mouth, placing her hands on Sylvia's ribs to see whether they expanded with the air she was providing. Nothing happened. Her convulsions had lessened, but this wasn't necessarily a good sign. Brera noticed that Sylvia's face was wet and thought, Why is she sweating so much?, then realized that she had soaked Sylvia's face with her own tears.

'The inhaler!'

She ran back into the house, through the living-room and into the hall. It was still on the floor. She picked it up and headed outside again. As she passed through the door on to the roof she shrieked.

Sylvia's body was seething and twitching. Twenty or thirty birds were sitting on her, covering her, smothering her. Brera threw herself at them, shouting, crying, and they ascended, together, like a funeral shroud, a brown feather blanket.

Sylvia's face was marked with large, red blotches. Brera took hold of her head and rammed the inhaler between her lips, but her teeth were clenched together now and grinding. She tried to

77

prise her jaw open but she wasn't strong enough. Instead she gathered her up in her arms, lifted her and, staggering, carried her through to the living-room. She dumped her on the couch, picked up the phone, dialled 999 and waited.

'Ambulance. Emergency. Jubilee Road, Hackney. Flat 9. Asthma. Please, quickly.'

She slammed down the receiver. What if they took too long? She had to get Sam.

She scrabbled among the pieces of paper next to the phone, hoping Sam had written Connor's number down. She saw a number written in Sam's hand and dialled it.

'Hello?'

It was Steven's number.

'Hi. Steven here.'

She thought her head was about to explode. She couldn't stop crying.

'Have you got a car? Where are you?'

'Who is this?'

'Brera. Please! Where are you?'

'I'm . . .'

'Are you near here? Are you near Hackney?'

'I . . . not far away. I'm at Liverpool Street. This is my mobile phone.'

Brera could hardly speak. 'Please come here. My daughter . . . I've phoned an ambulance but it might take too long. Please come.'

She dropped the receiver and ran back over to Sylvia. Sylvia was now limp, her eyes were closed and her head was lolling to one side. Brera lifted up her T-shirt and started to rub her chest. Sylvia's eyes opened slightly. She whispered, 'I'm not going anywhere.'

Brera felt as if a firework had gone off inside her mouth. 'You can bloody talk! You can bloody talk you little vixen and that's all you can say! You can talk and that's all you can say! Christ! Say something. No. Don't say anything. Just breathe!'

She stopped rubbing, ran out on to the roof, picked up the inhaler and sprinted back inside with it. She rammed it between

Sylvia's lips and pressed it three or four times. Most of the gas escaped through the sides of her mouth. Her head lolled. Brera tried it several more times and then, once again, attempted mouth to mouth.

It seemed like an age before she heard the buzzer sound. She ran to the entry-phone and pressed the button next to it, shoved the front door wide open to ease access and then ran to get Sylvia. She pulled down her T-shirt and tried to pick her up.

There was no ambulance, only Steven. He jogged up the stairs, through the flat, into the living-room. He was breathless and frightened, not so much by the possibility of facing something horrible (like a bloody injury, for example, a broken limb) as by the fear that he might not prove up to coping with it. He was prepared to see Sam, cut, bruised, maimed, electrocuted, but instead all he saw as he ran in was Brera, her face red, her hair red, wearing only a blue and white striped night-shirt, trying to pick up the prostrate body of a girl he had never seen before.

Brera glanced over her shoulder and saw, with horror, that it was only Steven. 'Oh God! I thought you were an ambulance. What good can you do? It's been at least fifteen minutes since I phoned.'

Steven moved swiftly over to Brera's side and helped her to lift the girl. He picked her up easily and held her in his arms. 'Shall I carry her downstairs? I can take you to casualty in my car, but you'll have to tell me where it is.'

The girl he held was trembling and wheezing. Her face was purple. He felt a wave of dizzyness at the prospect of carrying this sick creature, this sick thing, in his arms. She felt so light.

Brera completely lost control. She stood stiffly, blinking, saying nothing, clenching and unclenching her fists.

'Come on, let's go! Get a coat, or come as you are. I need you to give me directions.'

He turned and carried Sylvia towards the door. Brera ran after him. 'If we pass the ambulance on the way we can stop it.'

They reached the door and then all hell broke loose. Sylvia's body, previously slack and pliant, exploded out of Steven's arms like a firecracker.

'Let go of me!'

Steven tried to grab hold of her. Sylvia wasn't strong enough to resist, but she angled her body on the floor, against the two walls and the door, in such a way as to make moving her virtually impossible. When he tried to lunge at her, she kicked out at him, used her elbows and her nails.

He drew back. 'What's wrong with her? What is this?'

Brera ignored him, threw herself at Sylvia and landed on top of her, using all the force of her weight to subdue her. Steven looked on in amazement. He thought it possible that Brera might crush the girl completely, might certainly break a bone or a rib. He said, 'Don't hurt her . . . don't . . .'

Brera's weight curtailed Sylvia's thrashing. Her head collapsed to one side. Steven noticed, when this happened, that her nose was bleeding. The blood was dark. The sight of it appalled him.

Brera could hear noises on the stairs. Seconds later, two ambulancemen arrived carrying a stretcher. One of them had a bag and a syringe. Brera lifted herself. 'She's having an asthma attack but she won't leave the building. She's . . .'

No words for it. What was she?

The ambulanceman with the syringe said, 'Take her in and lay her down on a sofa.'

Brera scrambled up and grabbed hold of Sylvia's arms. Steven held her legs, and between them they carried her back to the sofa and dropped her on to it. Her body felt heavy, a dead weight. Her face was still purple, her lips were white and her teeth were chattering.

The ambulanceman filled his syringe, pulled up her sleeve, stuck it into her arm and emptied it. He then refilled the syringe and did the same thing again. 'What set this off? Some kind of allergy?'

Brera nodded.

'She should be hospitalized but I don't want to risk upsetting her any further,' he said.

'Maybe you could sedate her?'

'Too risky on top of the stuff I've just given her.'

Sylvia was moving her head from side to side. 'Just . . . bloody . . . leave me.'

He laughed. 'She can talk, but she can't breathe.' He peered into her face. 'How do you feel? Better yet?'

She didn't respond.

'How about we take you to hospital now? You'll be fine there.'

Sylvia's body, which had begun to relax, stiffened up again.

He opened his bag and took out an inhaler. He showed it to Brera. 'How much of this stuff has she had?'

'I don't know. A lot. But it didn't seem like she was breathing it in.'

'This close environment's setting her off. The weather especially. We have a nebulizer in the ambulance. It'll have to do her for the time being.'

Brera nodded. 'She had one before. If I keep her still for a few days and make her stay quiet . . .'

She leaned over the back of the sofa and spoke to Sylvia directly. 'You'll do as I say or I'll drag you to the hospital myself.'

Sylvia ignored her. The ambulanceman had refilled his syringe. He showed it to her. 'How are you feeling? Better? Do you want any more of this?'

She scowled up at him. Her face was still pale but less blotchy. Brera moved towards him, keen to help, feeling woefully inadequate for her earlier lack of competence. 'Can I do anything?'

'Make yourself a cup of tea.'

She nodded, chastened.

Steven said, 'I'll make the tea. I know where the kitchen is.'

Brera stared at Steven, looked at him as if she had only just realized that he was there, that it was *him*. She felt as if everyone was trying to make her feel useless, as though, in some way, this entire situation was her responsibility; Sylvia – her indomitable will, her obstinacy – had nothing whatsoever to do with it.

The ambulanceman felt Sylvia's pulse. 'Her heart's almost back to normal. She'll wheeze badly for a few days. She'll probably be very weak.'

He looked over at Brera. 'How old is she? Thirteen? Fourteen?'

'Nineteen. She just looks younger.'

'You'll have to be firm with her.'

She nodded, extremely resentful but incapable of expressing it. She wanted them all to go, then she would slap her, she could strangle her.

Of course she knew that she would do neither of these things. A cool bath and a packet of biscuits, she decided. They would have to suffice.

After carrying up the nebulizer, they set about rearranging the living-room furniture, pushing Sylvia, on the sofa, up against a wall so that the nebulizer could be placed next to a socket. As they worked a small congregation of birds accumulated on the window-sill. The door to the roof was still open and letting a cool breeze into the room; two or three birds were in the doorway. Brera, hawk-eyed, noticed them. She slammed the door and drew the curtains.

It was dark now. Sylvia turned her head and muttered something.

Brera moved closer, placing her ear next to Sylvia's lips. 'What?'

'Open the curtains.'

She frowned. 'Sorry?'

'Open the bloody curtains!'

Brera smiled. 'Open them yourself.'

Sylvia tried to move but she was too weak. She tried to speak again, but the ambulanceman gently placed the nebulizer mask across her nose and mouth. She stared at him, livid. What was he doing? He had gagged her. She closed her eyes. If she'd had the energy, she would have stopped breathing just to irritate him.

Later, after they'd gone, Brera sat in the kitchen with Steven and tried to explain. But Steven kept interjecting, to comment, to express sympathy and amazement.

When he was seventeen Steven had read the book *Sybil*, about a girl who'd had fourteen personalities. He'd also seen the film starring Sally Field. He said, 'This is twice as interesting as *Sybil*. You should write a story about it. Sell it.'

Brera frowned. 'This isn't like that. It isn't even very interesting. Only stupid. Stupid and sad.'

Steven was surprised by the ferocity in her voice. He said, 'Of course it's sad. I thought she was going to die back then. Just die as I stood there, holding her.'

Brera smiled at him, gently, wishing she owned a small firearm.

In the morning, bright and early, Ruby had taken the dog out for a long walk, down through Leicester Square, to the Embankment and along the river. This was now almost a habit, she decided, was already becoming one: last night, this morning. Thinking, walking. Couldn't be bad.

When she arrived back at the flat, Vincent was still stretched out on the sofa, half-asleep. She pulled open the curtains. He groaned. 'How early is it?'

She consulted her watch. 'Nine-forty-five. I'm working ten till six.'

He sat up. Ruby noticed that he was wearing a shirt. He was slightly chubby. His stomach protruded and his navel stuck out too, like a white cherry on an iced cup-cake.

'Why tell me that?'

'What?'

'Where you're going to be and how long.'

He yawned, not really expecting an answer.

She picked up a large, aluminium pan from the draining-board, rinsed it out and then threw some Weetabix, water and milk into it. This mixture she mashed up with a fork and then put down on the floor for the dog.

'Will you eat anything?' he asked, meaning by this that he would, that he wanted some coffee.

'I bought a cup of tea earlier.'

'You haven't chucked me out yet,' he said, secretly pleased, 'because you need me to stay.'

'Yeah?'

She watched the dog eating. She said, 'I don't want you feeding her or losing her. I'll put her muzzle on when she's finished her breakfast.'

He lay back down again, stretched out, pulled up his blanket. He debated whether he minded being indispensable, and decided that he didn't mind, on this particular occasion.

'You will be careful?'

'I will be.'

'There's dark glasses and a baseball hat in the bedroom. Unisex. In case you feel self-conscious.' How would he look without that mess on his face? She smiled to herself. Less colourful.

'Fine.'

'Don't step on her paws. I haven't paid for them yet.'

'So long as she doesn't step on mine.'

'I've paid for yours.'

'Ha!'

He waved at her. She completed her chores, patted the dog and left some spare keys in a prominent position.

When she'd gone, Vincent stared over the top of the sofa at Buttercup, who was sauntering around the kitchen area, sniffing the tiles through her muzzle. He whistled to her. She popped her head around the edge of the units and stared at him, obliging but sullen. He whistled again. She sat down.

He threw off his blankets and went into the bathroom for a pee. The dog followed him and watched from the doorway. Vincent flushed the toilet and then rinsed his face and hands in the sink. He stared at his wounds in the mirror and then debated whether to use Ruby's toothbrush, but didn't. Instead he ate some toothpaste, swallowed the foam and stepped over Buttercup, who was now lounging on her side, blocking the bathroom doorway.

He strolled into Ruby's bedroom and looked around for the hat and glasses she had mentioned. Eventually he found them, stuck on top of her wardrobe. He put them on and wandered into the living-room. The dog was now lying on the sofa.

He considered whether it was appropriate to play-wrestle with a greyhound. She seemed rather large. Just as he was forming an opinion on this issue the telephone rang. He answered it. 'Yes?'

There was a pause. It was Steven.

'This is Ruby's flat,' Vincent said smartly, 'but she's not here.' As he spoke, he picked up the packet of Weetabix, took one out and ate it dry.

'She's at work?'

Vincent's mouth was full. There was a short pause and then Steven said, 'I met you, didn't I? The other night.'

Vincent couldn't remember. Dreamworld, he thought, Dreamland.

'Will you just tell her that it's off tomorrow. There's been a hitch, so it's off.'

'Fine.'

'You will tell her?'

'Yes. Fine.'

He chewed on the cereal, his mouth a cement-mixer, turning, churning, his brain, already, he decided, a cool block of concrete.

Steven hung up. He turned and stared over at Sylvia, who was lying on the couch, almost obscured by darkness, wheezing.

Eventually he said, 'I'm Steven, by the way, if you can hear me.'

Sylvia said nothing. She felt absolutely miserable. She just kept thinking, They all patronize me. Why won't they leave me? I wish I was strong enough to chuck a chair at this fool. Even a pillow, but a pillow isn't hard enough. I couldn't aim properly anyway. It's too dark. And she felt so tired.

Connor had agreed to rehearse without the use of amplifiers. Sam and Sarah were sitting in the kitchen discussing Sarah's work.

Sarah was shouting above the noise, 'Men have always linked the female sex with a kind of irrationality. Hysteria is perceived as something entirely feminine. Doctors used to think that when a woman became hysterical her womb rose into her throat and became jammed there. Men get hysterical all the time but we just don't use the same words to describe their anger. Of course it's exactly the same anger. Sensitivity, hypersensitivity, mysticism, magic. These are all things that marginalize us. But women

85

pretend to enjoy the margins. It's a kind of control through a lack
of control, if you see what I mean. We're responsible for our own
contradictions.'

In the next room, Connor started to drum in earnest, then to
sing. Sam stuck a finger in each ear. Sarah followed suit. They
grinned at each other, dumbly.

Ruby was sitting on the sofa watching *This is Your Life* and
waiting impatiently for Vincent to return with the dog. She'd
been rattling around in the flat for an hour or so, aimless, like a
pea in a tin can. She was trying not to worry over his whereabouts, and took reassurance from the fact that his shirt was still
on the floor. It smelled – she noticed when she sniffed it – of
sweat and vomit.

When he let himself in she said, 'I tried to phone you earlier
this morning but you'd gone already.'

This sounded like an accusation, but he didn't let it bother him.
He felt a general sense of well-being, was pleased, in fact, to see
Ruby, although he was uncertain why. He smiled at her. 'I've been
exercising this dog all day. I haven't rested for a single minute.'

There was something speculative and unfinished about his
speech. She said, 'I only asked you to look after her,' and made a
kissing noise at the dog, patting her lap to encourage her over.
Buttercup strolled across and sat down next to Ruby, sniffing at
her legs through the muzzle. She had a strangely replete air
about her.

'You didn't feed her, did you?'

Vincent shook his head, taking a rucksack off his shoulder and
slinging it on the floor. 'She chewed a cigarette butt, only she
didn't swallow it.'

'You've been drinking.'

He ignored her. 'What'll you feed her tonight?'

Ruby stroked the dog between her ears. 'She should be eating
a special high-fibre diet. Stuff called Beta-Racer. I couldn't find
any, though, so I got her some normal dog food instead.'

Vincent sat down on the sofa next to her. She stared at his
profile. 'Your bruises are still bad.'

86

He nodded and then stretched out his legs and pushed his hands into the pockets of his jeans. He pulled out a handful of notes. 'Here.'

She took the notes and counted them: Two tens and four twenties. 'What's this? Where did you get it?'

He leaned forward and stroked the dog. Ruby noticed with some alarm how natural this gesture looked. She couldn't help thinking how useful the dog was, as an excuse, as a reason to ignore everything.

'Did you borrow it?'

'I won it in a bet, in a pub.'

She rolled the notes up into a tight wad. 'It's illegal to bet with people you don't know in pubs. You can get arrested for it.'

He smiled. 'I'd fucking burp and they'd have me for noise pollution.'

Her eyes returned to the television screen. 'I'm just telling you.'

After a short pause he said, 'You'll be needing some new sunglasses.'

'You lost them?'

He shook his head.

'You broke them?'

'No. I ate them.'

She focused on his face. 'You ate them?'

He nodded. 'For a bet.'

'I bought those on the Kings Road. I liked them.'

'I only ate the lenses. The frame was still intact, but I couldn't see any point in bringing that back.'

'You'll be ill again.'

'I won't. I vomited them up straight away.'

'You hate vomiting.'

'I hate a lot of things, but I still do most of them.'

The money. She felt it in her hand. What was he after?

They both stared at the television for a while. Eventually she said, 'You didn't do anything special with the hat, then?'

He picked up his bag. The hat was squeezed into one of the front compartments. He pulled it out and tossed it at her. It landed on her lap and she stared at it without moving. He pulled open the main flap of the rucksack, took out a record from the back and passed it to her. She took it from him and pulled the corners of the cover straight where they had become bent in the course of his journey. Ray Charles. It wasn't new.

'This is a completely different record. Thanks, anyway.'

He located his toothbrush in his bag and sprang up. 'I'm just going to brush my teeth.'

She handed him the roll of notes. 'Stick these into the coffee jar in the cupboard above the sink.'

After he'd done as she'd instructed he went into the bathroom.

She wondered where the rucksack had come from. What exactly had he been doing all day? The dog looked all right. Tired, though. She picked up one of her paws. The pads looked fine.

Vincent returned and sat back down on the sofa. 'What's this about?' He was holding the registration booklet.

'Bad news.'

'Why?'

'Read it.'

Inside he found a betting slip; on it, some notes. 'I wrote those today,' she said, 'in a spare moment.'

'Is she any good at racing?'

'She came in the first three during her maiden race, which I think is good. But she's raced badly since.'

'How many races?' He looked at the book.

'Too many. She could race well if she felt like it, but she doesn't seem to want to.'

He inspected her betting slip. 'What's this mean?'

'Things that might help. I listed them.' She pointed. 'That says "weight".'

'She needs to lose a few pounds? Well, that's straightforward enough.' He battled to read on: 'Hurdles, handicap, distance and positioning.'

'She hasn't raced over hurdles before. I thought she might be good at it.'

He frowned. 'If she can't be bothered running in a normal race, how's making her jump things going to help?'

'It's complicated.'

She stood up and went into the kitchen, opened a bag of dog biscuits and tipped them on to a plate.

Vincent was still reading her notes. 'What does handicap mean?'

She picked up a can opener and stuck it into the top of a tin. 'Sometimes she interferes with other dogs. That's a really bad sign. Greyhounds aren't bred to be aggressive. Bitches especially. So if you have a greyhound that snaps at other dogs – even though it's usually only because of friendliness or boredom – the racing manager gets really upset about it.'

'I asked about the handicap.'

'Well, if she ran in a handicap race her trap would be at the front. Because she's crap they'd give her a head start.'

'And so?'

'When she's released she'd have the advantage of a few extra seconds on her side. She'd be able to see the hare without being put off by other dogs.'

'You've written "positioning" here in capital letters.'

'Yep. It's connected.'

She mashed up the meat from the tin with the biscuits, put the bowl down for the dog and took off the muzzle. 'I bought two bits of fish on the market this afternoon. Maybe you could make dinner?'

'I know that some dogs run wide and some run close to the fence.'

'The rails.' She grinned.

Vincent caught her expression. 'Well, fuck you!'

She walked back over and sat down again. 'OK.'

He pushed his toothbrush behind his ear, as if it were a pen, and folded his arms.

'There are six traps. The first four traps are chosen in a kind of draw. The first trap is usually the best trap for most dogs because the distance that dog ends up running is much shorter, I mean, if it stays close to the rails.'

'Why?'

'Think about it. The dogs run an oval course. The inside of an oval is going to be a shorter distance than the outside. Anyway, if a dog is a good railer and a fast trapper and it's in trap one, it'll be hard to beat. In the bookies, if anyone's going to bet in forecast doubles, most punters will bet the combination one and six. They're the two best traps.'

'Why six, then? The dog in that trap'd be running the longest distance.'

Ruby nodded. 'True. The two outside traps, five and six, aren't included in the draw. Dogs that are well-known wide runners are always given the outside traps to save on injuries.'

He was frowning again. Ruby jumped up and hunted around for a pen and some paper. She found a small red pen and the back of an electricity bill. She sat down and drew a large oval and then six small boxes on the oval which she numbered one to six, then moved up closer to Vincent to show him what she was doing. He felt her leg touching his, could smell her hair.

'If a wide runner was placed in any of the four inside tracks, he'd come powering out when the trap opened and go shooting towards the hare, smacking into several other dogs in the process. The speed they go, he'd probably end up hurting either himself or one of the other runners. What it comes down to is the fact that a wide runner will always chase the hare.'

'Hold on . . .' He was confused. 'So if they're all chasing the hare, what about the railer, the dog in trap one?'

She smiled. 'Dogs are like people. They do stuff for different reasons. The strains of dogs from which most of today's greyhounds are bred were strains that just ran for the sake of it. They'll chase anything. For a railer, it's more the running than the chasing that excites them. If a dog is a good railer, then it isn't that bothered about catching the hare. It's canny. It knows how to win a race.'

'So,' Vincent took the pen off her and pointed it at the two boxes numbered five and six, 'what about these dogs? They're just stupid?'

'Nope. The distance around the track is longer from these two traps, but at the same time they've got much more room to really stretch out. Racing's all about negotiating bends. A dog that's railing has a much tighter bend to negotiate, and the other dogs will be crowding him more. But the wide runner can really stride out and he's less likely to be bumped.'

Vincent rubbed his forehead. Ruby noticed. 'It gets even more complicated when you try and think how your own animal fits into the whole thing.'

Buttercup had finished her dinner and was now lying across the kitchen tiles. Vincent turned his head and stared at her. 'What sort of a runner is she?'

Ruby took hold of the registration booklet, opened it, pointed. 'That there is the first race she ran. Her time . . .' She ran her finger down the column, calculating out loud. 'She was at least five or six seconds faster in that race than in any of her others.'

'Which trap?'

'Two. Which makes you think she's going to be a railer, but in fact I know she runs fairly wide. She's never been in traps five or six, but they've run her in all the others and she hasn't done anything.'

Vincent was staring at Ruby's ear as she spoke. He said, 'Did you have all those holes made in your ear at the same time?'

'What?'

She frowned at him. He scratched his nose. 'If you think about it, there's no point in considering this stuff tactically unless you've actually seen the race.'

She closed the book. 'And how d'you work that one out?'

'Well, a race isn't only about how one dog performs.'

'But I'm only interested in one dog.'

'I'm saying that a race isn't about how one dog performs, it's about how six dogs perform. Maybe she is a wide runner.'

'So why her best performance from trap two?'

'Well, maybe in that race she came out of the trap faster than the other dogs to her right, was able to see the hare, unhindered, and move outside before the other dogs overtook her.'

Ruby thought about this. 'I don't think she's a particularly fast trapper, which means she doesn't usually come out of the trap all that quickly.'

She threw the book down and stood up. 'I'd better get dinner on.'

'So what's the plan?'

'Fish.'

'Not for dinner, for the dog.'

He stretched out his arms across the back of the sofa; his fingers nearly reached her as she leaned on the arm. 'You've written out your lists and you said she's got a race on Thursday.'

Ruby stared at her finger-nails. She was wearing a transparent polish that made them shine, but they still looked ragged.

He said, 'I think we should take her down to the track right now and experiment.'

'How? What good would that do?'

'You've got to offer her some kind of incentive.'

'Like what?'

'Greyhound racing originated with coursing, didn't it? Dogs chasing live hares?'

'In Ireland.'

'She's probably just bored. She isn't stimulated, so she won't perform.'

Ruby shook her head. 'I was telling you how these strains of dogs chase anything. Usually they'll run after anything because that's how they're bred.'

'So?'

She thought for a moment. 'In coursing I know for a fact that dogs never interfere with each other.'

'Why's that?'

'Lots of reasons.'

Vincent grinned. 'Deviants are always more intelligent, so they get bored more easily.'

Ruby considered this for a while. Eventually she said, 'We can't just go down to the track. They might have speedway on tonight. Anyway, I'm tired and she's just eaten.'

'In the morning, then.'

She stood up. 'I suppose I could phone and ask if it's all right to take her down early.'

'If we get there for eight, you'd have a full two hours before work.'

Ruby went to the phone and picked up the receiver. She didn't feel very enthusiastic herself, but any enthusiasm, from any source, no matter how misplaced, was better than none at all. She was about to dial and then stopped.

'Why all this sudden interest in the dog? I didn't know you even liked dogs.'

He was staring at the television. 'I don't. But I do like plans.'

Ideas. To have an idea, he thought. To think and to do. What could be better?

She stared suspiciously at the back of his head before dialling. He was full of shit.

Sam sipped her lager and waved a hand in front of her face. Someone nearby was smoking and holding their cigarette too close. She shouted, 'Well, everything's relative, isn't it? I mean, your position is always going to be affected by where you stand, who you are and your sex.'

She couldn't help thinking how smart Sarah looked. Her hair was drawn back away from her face and she wore very little make-up, except for black liquid eye-liner on her top lids and some mascara which made her eyes look enormous. Sam couldn't believe she'd managed to persuade her to come along tonight. She felt honoured.

Sarah put her lips close to Sam's ear: 'Yeah, that's fair enough, but sometimes that sort of argument gets you out of everything, if you see what I mean. Relativism's often just an excuse for not committing.'

She was stopped, mid-flow, by someone pushing past her who tipped up her drink. It spilled down her shirt and drenched her breasts. She swore and tried to wring it out ineffectually with one hand. 'It's too bloody full in here,' she shouted, 'and it's too LOUD.'

Sam grabbed hold of her arm and steered her towards the nearest exit. 'It shouldn't stain if you give it a quick rub down.'

Sarah indicated the stage with her hand. 'Won't Connor be on soon? It's been at least half an hour since the last lot played.'

'They'll be doing loads of songs. I don't think we're obliged to see every one.'

Sam threaded a route around the bar, towards the ladies' toilets.

Inside were two or three women. It was cramped, even in here. Sam turned on the warm tap at one of the sinks and beckoned Sarah over. 'Splash some water over it. There's some liquid soap if you want it. Then hold it under the hand dryer.'

Sarah tried to bend over the sink. 'It's right down the front. I'll end up even wetter this way.'

Outside Sam could hear the taped music stop and a loud cheer as people waited for the imminent arrival of the band on-stage. She said, 'I've always really hated this place, but it must be exciting to play here. Connor's played here loads.'

She walked to the door and opened it, standing on tip-toe to try to see the stage. But the crowds were too dense and her angle too oblique. The three women who had been in the toilet repairing their make-up and brushing their hair pushed past her. Sarah shouted from inside, 'What's happening?'

She walked back in. 'They've come on. I can't see them, though, only hear them.'

Sarah cocked her head to one side and listened. 'I can just hear a kind of roaring noise. Is it them or the toilet cistern?'

Sam grinned. 'You must be so glad you came.'

Outside there was more cheering.

'What are they called again?'

Sam watched with surprise as Sarah unbuttoned her shirt and took it off.

'Stirsign.'

She held it under the tap, lathering it with soap and then rinsing it.

Sam watched her. 'D'you want me to stand guard at the door?'

'Not when the band's just come on. It's perfectly private in here.'

She wrung out the shirt and then stuck it under the hand dryer.

Sam couldn't help staring at Sarah's body, which was pale, angular and extremely thin. She wore a turquoise bra which efficiently cupped her small, neat breasts. Sam thought her too thin, as though if she moved too sharply or quickly her bones might push through the skin and show themselves, bursting out like little daggers.

Sam touched Sarah's shirt to see how quickly it was drying. 'It's still soaking. The dryer isn't very efficient.'

Sarah misconstrued the source of Sam's concern. 'Look, why don't you go on out? I wouldn't want you to miss anything.'

Sam shook her head. 'I can see him any time. Anyway, it's too crowded out there.'

'What's your star sign?'

'Guess.'

'Aquarius or Gemini.'

'Neither: Pisces, but I am a water sign, if that's what you're getting at.'

Sarah smiled at this. 'I'm a fire sign. We're incompatible.'

Sam was about to reply when the door swung open and two women came in. She noticed them staring at Sarah's bare skin and exchanging glances. One of them went into a cubicle while the other fluffed up her hair with her hands, watching Sarah in the mirror. Sam felt compromised, but couldn't understand why.

'D'you want me to hold it under for a while?'

Sarah, apparently oblivious, handed the shirt over. 'Thanks.'

She picked up her lager and took a sip of it. Sam held the shirt under the dryer. It felt soft.

The second girl came out of the cubicle, washed her hands and then held them, dripping, limply in front of her.

'Oh, sorry.'

Sam turned and was about to step sideways. But Sarah said, 'Don't worry,' pushed her firmly up against the dryer and kissed her, fully.

Sarah's lips felt delicate and her breath tasted of lager and another flavour: garlic or liquorice. Sam felt Sarah's tongue, like a mollusc, a foreign thing, curving up along the inside of her lips.

She felt her hands, she was sure she felt them, touching her breasts, soft on her breasts. The dryer pushed out warm air, the weight of them both reactivating its mechanism.

Just as suddenly, Sarah withdrew. She was laughing. 'They've gone. We frightened the shit out of them. Give me my shirt and I'll put it on.'

Sam handed her the shirt. 'Why did you do that?'

Sarah slipped it on and began to fasten the buttons. 'It was the highlight of their evening.'

She peered at herself in the mirror, wiped the corners of her lips with her thumb and forefinger, smiled and then pushed the door open, holding it ajar for Sam. 'Come on.'

Sam didn't pause to check her own reflection. *Her stomach*. How did it feel? As if she'd just been told the lemonade she'd been drinking was actually turpentine. A kind of horror. Confusion? No. A pure feeling without fixed meaning.

Sarah led the way, pushing past people at the back, moving gradually forwards. Near the front, everyone was dancing. Several people were stage diving.

Sam shouted over the noise, 'If we get too close we'll get thrown about. Everyone's pushing.'

Sarah launched herself into the middle of the fray. Sam opted to stay back, craning her neck, trying to see Connor. Eventually she could see him, banging away at his drum-kit, hair in his face, T-shirt still on but soaking wet.

I want to feel part of this, she thought. She wanted to, but suddenly she felt removed from everything. Lonely. Alone. The drum, the beat, the sound it made, reminded her. Of what?

She was twelve years old and Sylvia was asking her if she could borrow her skipping rope. The music – she couldn't escape it, but she could block it – came in waves. It reminded her of the rope: swinging round and round, whizzing, whirring and slapping the ground.

Sylvia had borrowed it. Sam heard the rope turning: vicious, unstoppable, cyclical. She watched Sylvia's feet as she jumped, inefficiently shod in a pair of old, soft, blue canvas deck shoes.

Sylvia counted as she jumped, 'One, two, three, four . . .' By the time she'd reached fifty, her feet had grown heavier, faltering. She stopped on fifty-four, without grace, clumsily tangled, her breathing laboured.

On the ground, surrounding her, their necks and wings broken, were five or six birds. Injured by the rope. Killed by the rope.

Sylvia fell to her knees and gathered them up with her hands, her breath turning into jerky tears.

Sam had watched coldly, thinking, Will I ever love anything that much?

Her heart contracted and the feeling she experienced was not so much love as jealousy.

Steven spent the evening watching *Sophie's Choice* on video. During any especially tedious or gut-wrenching moments he cast an eye, somewhat apathetically, over the latest edition of *The Stage*.

Steven loved Meryl Streep. If asked to explain this adoration, he'd say that he loved the way that she was never shrewish. She was so dignified. She could be angry – he thought she did Angry extremely well – but she was never vulgar. She didn't forget herself, her dignity.

Sometimes he'd masturbate as he watched her on screen. She was so aloof, and that in itself was sexy. But after he'd finished – when he'd cleared away the tissues and washed his hands – he'd always feel an intense pang of self-disgust.

He'd been staring at one particular page of *The Stage* for several minutes, reading but not reading, when something caught his eye and caused him to blink, pick up the paper and stare at it more intently. The focus of his attention was a small but nicely written obituary towards the bottom of the page. He read it, re-read it.

Sylvia watched Brera talking on the phone. She watched but she didn't listen. She'd been using the nebulizer since the morning, and its vapours had been opening her bronchial tubes, releasing the hostage air in her lungs, and then escaping; travelling onwards, upwards, making her brain smart, glisten, pulsate, making colours painfully clear, and smells . . . but she couldn't smell anything, she just knew that everything was clearer, magnified, extended, elongated. Her senses were ecstatically jumbled.

Brera was sitting close by, talking on the phone but also staring at Sylvia, thinking, It's not so much that she can't breathe, more that she doesn't want to breathe. She's happier not breathing.

She focused on Sylvia's face. Her lips were moving, she was muttering, and whenever the mask fell from her nose and mouth, Brera could hear disjointed pieces of conversation. She struggled to keep her attention focused on Steven.

Inside Sylvia's head facts and images were floating, connecting, disconnecting. She said, 'I can see these conversations taking place, everywhere, but really the conversation is the same one. It's the same conversation.'

She saw herself in a place full of bright lights and a bright girl with white hair was saying something about ideas.

'You say you like ideas? What does that mean?'

A voice responded. It came from nowhere, but it was a harsh voice, full of emphasis: 'Ideas alter things, form things, change things unilaterally. They can be modified, disciplined, controlled. I see stuff. Life. I see life and it's only a mishmash of facts, thoughts, images, pictures. But everything crystallizes in my head, forms doctrine, produces its own clear meaning. My mind works that way.'

Sylvia couldn't understand this at all. The girl seemed to be having difficulty too, but she said, 'Life is more jumbled than you think. Caring about things should be enough. Even if you can only manage to care about one thing. You have to understand what it is to be good. Not so much what you can make of life, but what you can give to it.'

Sylvia wasn't bothered any more, but the dialogue continued anyway. 'That's an idea, though! It's just that you can't be bothered to take it any further, to politicize. It's just sloppy thinking.'

Sylvia could taste the word *politicize* on her tongue. Its rough edges, its sharpness. She had no feelings either way – towards it or against it – she could only taste it.

The white voice was saying, 'I never take things further because that's how you get into trouble. Once you accept one thing, you end up accepting loads of stuff, half of which you don't really understand. When things get too big, they get out of your control. You start off by thinking that you're being good, but you end up finding out that ideas have a life of their own. They can turn bad, can make you bad and you don't even know it.'

The hard face, the hard voice, laughed. This laughter tickled Sylvia. It had its own particular charm, this laugh, like snuff, or the smell of fruity pipe tobacco. 'But I want to get into trouble! Don't you? Why not get into trouble? You're naïve. You know it too, and you think that your naivety makes you good, but in fact all it makes you is easy to manipulate.'

'Manipulate? Who by?'

'By me. By anyone and everyone.'

Sylvia felt herself being sucked away and thrown between the stars, but the stars were on the ceiling, were, in fact, just one star: a bright bulb peeking through a wicker shade. The roof was white. Now she heard something else, but it was the same thing she had heard before. A familiar voice, but a different place, in a sea of orange and roughness: 'I'm like you. I like to think about things, to be open to every influence and then to make up my mind. But sometimes, sometimes it becomes impossible to make up your mind because the information, the information . . . books, paper, pens, books, films, paper, pens . . .'

Sylvia digested the word *information* and it made her want to burp. The voice said 'information' almost as though it had not said that word at all but had said 'sex' – with a mixture of desire and dread. 'Sometimes you end up finding out too much. Reading, discovering and uncovering.'

Sylvia wanted to locate the other half of this conversation, thought for one awful second that she herself was expected to provide it. Luckily this was not so. The voice came, the rebuttal. It was a loving voice, wheedling and whining: 'You don't have to digest everything, to crystallize it. Why can't you just open yourself up to things, be open to things and let that be an end in itself? I guess that's a sort of, a kind of . . .' The voice hesitated. 'I was going to say "liberalism", but I don't want to involve myself in all that.'

The first voice sounded sad: 'That's just it. You have to involve yourself, otherwise you can't give anything.'

'I want peace and freedom.'

'Clichés.'

'Why?'

'Because those things don't mean anything when you say them.'

Sylvia picked up the word *mean* and juggled with it. She thought, Everything has meaning. I'm in a sea of it. Swimming in it, drowning.

The voices came together in her head and each voice she tried to simplify by making it into a shape. The harsh voice became a square, the white voice an arrow, the familiar voice was a circle . . . A fifth voice emerged, strident, sensual, suggestive, feminine. It said, 'I don't want truth. Ideas get lost in truth. Truth is stupid. Take any letter away from it and it becomes stupid. *Trut. Thur. Hutt. Ruth.* It's just a word. It's just another word and words stand for very little unless you use them sensibly and with rigour. I only want truth if I can use it. I want to rebuild the world with my own ideas, selectively.'

This voice contained all of the other shapes. It was a star. It throbbed. For a horrible moment Sylvia thought that this was in fact her voice, her own voice, but then she realized that she didn't believe anything that this voice was saying. She mistrusted it. She had no voice herself.

Ideas flooded the room and she floated on them. One idea was that every story was one story, everything boiled down into one single narrative. Every thought, idea, commentary, fiction, was travelling towards a single meaning. She tried to find this meaning but it was hopeless. It was too big. It was nothing. That one meaning might have to be God, she decided, which would be like a defeat.

She found herself in a cave. She remembered reading *A Passage to India* (where did that come from?) and the sequence in the caves, with the echo, when every noise that was made, that could be made, every noise was reduced to nothing, a hauntingly meaningless echo, a jolt, a thud.

A song became a thud, a poem became a thud, a prayer became a thud, a sneeze, a thud, science, thud, beauty, thud, glory, thud, love, thud, God . . . And so . . .

She sighed. The mask fell from her face and she, in turn, fell from dreaming to sleeping.

Brera put down the phone and walked over to Sylvia. She picked up the mask, folded it and turned off the nebulizer at the plug. The air smelled high and vaporous. She stared down at her sleeping daughter, then slowly, hollowly, said out loud the worst word she could think of: 'Cunt.'

She regretted this instantly. 'Sam would have something to say about why I chose that word,' she muttered. 'I'm too old to swear.'

It didn't even make her feel better. It just sounded foolish.

TWELVE

Connor woke Sam by kissing her ribs and her belly, by dampening her hips with tiny, sharp licks and bites.

Unfortunately, as Sam awoke, instead of finding this luxurious introduction to wakefulness pleasurable and erotic, she had to restrain the impulse to slap Connor with the back of her hand, to swat him.

'Did we argue last night?' she asked.

Connor's tongue stopped what it was doing and he straightened up, placing his head next to hers on the pillow. He stared at her, but she didn't catch his expression because she was looking up at the ceiling.

'I don't think we did. I was drunk. I remember Sarah droning on about something.'

'What's the time?'

She could smell his hair, which, although it looked ragged and uncombed, was soft on her shoulder and smelled of smoke from the night before.

'I dunno. Eight? Eight-thirty?'

She sat bolt upright. 'I promised Brera I'd be home early today. We're going shopping.'

Connor grinned. 'Oh yeah?'

She looked down at him. 'You can't come.'

'Why?' He pretended to be hurt.

'Because I'm going with Brera.'

'Sounds weird when you call her by her name.'

He reached down and pinched her knee, then let his hand slip up and along the inside of her thigh. She leaned over, pecked his cheek and jumped out of bed. 'Actually, I would invite you to come, but I know you've got an interview at lunchtime.'

'Which leaves me four hours to think of something interesting to say.'

'You think that's long enough?'

He laughed and threw a pillow at her, but she ducked and padded through to the kitchen.

Sarah was lounging against the kitchen cabinets waiting for the kettle to boil, wearing a short, multi-coloured bathrobe. Her long thin legs protruded from the robe, untanned. As she leaned over, Sam could see the curve of her breast and her tiny, pink nipple. Sarah's red hair had fallen across her face, half covering it.

'Hello.'

Sarah turned, straightened herself, and pulled a handful of curls behind her ear. 'I'm totally knackered. Jet lag.'

She yawned with neat precision, like a cat.

'Making coffee?' Sam asked.

'Tea.'

Sam walked over to the kettle and turned it off at the plug before it had a chance to boil for too long.

'Mine's white, if you're making. I like it insipid.'

Sam busied herself locating cups and finding a tea-bag. She wasn't sure if she felt a tension between them. She thought, Maybe it's just because she isn't dressed. She's so sluttish, the way she lounges about. No make-up, her face all gaunt and white.

'Do you have any plans for today?' She poured water on to Sarah's tea-bag.

Sarah shrugged, noncommital. 'You?'

'I've got to go shopping with my mother. We're having some photos taken this afternoon.'

Sarah's face brightened. 'Can I come?'

'It'll be very dull.'

'Go on. It'll be a laugh. I can meet your mother. That'd be interesting.'

Sam finished making the two coffees. 'I'll phone and ask once I've taken this in to Connor.'

Sarah poured some extra milk into her tea. 'I hope he appreciates you running around after him like this.'

Sam said nothing, only smiled as she carried the cup carefully out of the kitchen.

Connor reached out for the cup. Sam perched on the edge of the bed and handed it to him. 'Can I use the phone?'

'Sure.'

He pulled himself up into a sitting position, careful not to spill anything.

'Sarah wants to come shopping.'

He frowned. 'Why?'

'I don't know. She said she thought it'd be fun.'

'Amusing. I bet she said she thought it'd be amusing. That's the kind of thing she'd say.'

'She said she thought it'd be a laugh.'

He brushed some hair out of his eyes. 'Will she be going back to the flat in Hackney with you?'

'Does it matter?'

He seemed to think that it did.

'Have you told her about Sylvia?' Her name felt strange on his tongue, as though it implied a familiarity that didn't in fact exist.

'No. Why? Should I discuss my sister with everyone? I'm sure you don't make a habit of discussing your family at length with every new person you meet.'

'I'm just saying that you hardly know her.'

Sam stared at him, irritated. 'I hardly knew you once and it wasn't a problem.'

Connor put his cup of coffee on the carpet and lay back down in bed. How can I feel jealous? he thought. Of *her*. Christ.

'I'm tired,' he said, sullenly.

'Fine.' She stood up. 'You're being pathetic.'

He didn't answer. She pulled on her clothes, picked up her coat, which was slung over the door handle, and closed the door gently behind her.

Sarah was getting dressed in her bedroom. The door was slightly ajar. Sam called through: 'I'm ready to go when you are.'

Sarah appeared in the doorway wearing an old-fashioned,

yellow shirtwaister, black tights and flat black shoes. Her hair was tied back with a yellow scarf. She wore no make-up.

'That didn't take long. The dress is great.'

'Did you phone your mother?'

Sam shook her head. 'No, but I shouldn't think she'll be bothered.'

Sam followed Sarah out of the flat. 'I didn't mention my sister before, did I?'

'No. She sing too?'

'Not much. We let her write some of our music.'

Sarah slammed the front door. 'Yeah?'

'She suffers from a kind of disability.'

'Really?'

Sam stepped out into the street. 'She's afflicted.'

'An affliction?' Sarah smiled. 'Sounds biblical.'

As soon as he heard the front door slam, Connor sat up in bed and looked frantically around his bedroom, trying to locate something – anything – that Sam might have left behind. Eventually his eyes settled on a small, white, cotton bra which was slung over the cymbal on his drum-kit. He went and picked it up, then folded it carefully so that it would fit into the fist of one hand. He smiled to himself, feeling its softness, then stopped smiling and tried to bring to mind exactly what it was that had passed between them.

Vincent led the way down to Berwick Street. He was bossy this morning and full of purpose. 'I'm sure I saw a butcher's down here.'

Ruby nodded. 'There's a few of them. They all open early. Supply hotels and stuff.'

'This one.'

They went inside. Vincent smiled at the butcher, who stared at him coldly, taking in, in one glance, the cut on his forehead and his crumpled shirt.

'I want a whole rabbit.'

'Skinned?'

'No, whole. Ears, fur, everything.'

The butcher disappeared into the rear of the shop. When he had gone Vincent turned to Ruby: 'I used to do this trick with dead rabbits when I was a kid. I'll show you later.'

She imagined him as a child – exactly the same, only smaller. She wondered what he was up to, but didn't really care. She'd given up on things, temporarily. He'd had that effect on her.

Outside again, he said, 'We want to head for Oxford Street.'

'Fine. We can catch the bus from Oxford Circus.'

Oxford Street was quiet at this hour. Vincent stopped walking and leaned against a rubbish bin. They stood in silence together.

'Now what?'

'Shut up and listen.'

She waited mutely for several minutes but nothing happened. The dog began to grow impatient and pulled on her lead. She was about to complain when Vincent said, 'I can hear something. Can you hear it? The dog can.'

Ruby looked down at Buttercup and as she looked she began to hear something: a strange kind of clattering and banging, a hollow noise, a repetitive thuddering-shuddering. Like thunder. Like an earthquake. She stared down the street, towards Oxford Circus and gasped.

A sea of horses. So huge. A glorious plague of them. Filling the city, exploding its damp, grey glass and granite, its rubble, its tarmac. Shattering the city with the gloss of fur, of muscle. Steam; ears, nostrils, quivering; eyes, black, whites rolling; tassels; tails. The smell of them. Their froth, their breath, their foam. Saddle leather. Sweet wax.

This was beauty. Like a knife twisting in her stomach. They passed her by, three abreast, on and on and on. Until the last, like water trickling down a plug hole, suddenly gone. Like a drum that stops beating. Beating.

'It's a fascist thing, really.'

'What?' She could still hardly breathe.

'That feeling.'

Her eyes were full of tears. He had given her this moment, had handed it to her. She said, 'Don't say anything else. You'll ruin it.'

106

He laughed at her – she was such a fool – and walked down to Oxford Circus, still laughing.

They stood on the track.

'What's the plan, then?'

He looked around him. 'Give me a minute.' Then added, 'Let's walk her for a while.'

'Great idea.'

He scowled at her, but they started walking. Vincent had been full of ideas the night before, full of plans and schemes, all of which had suddenly dissolved.

Ruby was saying, 'Either they feel the urge or they don't.'

'Where's the hare?'

She stood still and glanced around the perimeter of the track. 'If we carry on walking we're bound to come across it.'

They walked past the traps, six metal boxes, neatly numbered, which had been pushed off the sandy track and on to the grass verge.

'How come the traps aren't on the track?'

'They're mobile. Think about it. If they left the traps on the track after a race had started, the dogs'd run into them on the last bend.'

'Can we push them out?'

They pushed them out together. Vincent wanted to put Buttercup into one.

Ruby opened trap six and helped her inside. Vincent walked around to the front and peered in at her. He could see her pointed nose and her eyes. 'She looks pretty bored from this end.'

Ruby crossed her arms. 'She's bound to. She can't hear the hare or anything.'

'Can we run her now?'

'No. I'd have to ask the groundsman to operate the hare and I don't fancy doing that.'

She opened the trap, pulled the dog out and put her lead back on. 'The hare's over there. Can you see it?'

Vincent looked in the direction she had indicated. 'That orange and white thing? It's like a balloon. No wonder she can't be bothered chasing it.'

He walked over and inspected it more closely, then took his rabbit out of the plastic bag, holding it aloft in his left hand, pushing the hare manually along its runner with his right, so that it made the requisite clattering noise.

The dog's ears pricked up and she pulled on her leash. Ruby held her back. Vincent continued pushing and after several steps he broke into a slow trot. The dog began to bark and pulled on her lead so hard that Ruby had to hold on to it with both hands.

'She's pulling my arms off.'

Vincent carried on jogging but shouted over his shoulder, 'Keep her until I tell you, then let her come, but let her pull you.'

The dog was riding up on to her back legs, still barking. Twenty yards on, he shouted, 'Come on, then!'

Ruby allowed the dog to pull her along, slowly at first, but after several steps she could no longer control her and moved faster, and then faster still. Eventually she was running after Vincent and the dog was loping in slow but effortless bounds. Vincent stopped the hare just beyond the finishing line, about sixty yards from its original position.

He was breathless. He tossed his brown rabbit across the artificial hare and waited for Ruby and the dog to catch up.

'What shall I do?' Ruby was hurtling towards him.

'Let her have it.'

She couldn't do otherwise. The dog jerked out of her hands, almost pulling her arm from its socket, charged at the rabbit and did her best to grab hold of it through her muzzle. She managed, somehow, to snatch it off the hare and shook it, swinging her head violently from side to side. The fur on the rabbit's hindquarters started to rip and the red flesh gaped through. Vincent, exhausted, was roaring with laughter. Ruby was bent double, trying to catch her breath, feeling the palm of her hand burning from the pull of the leash.

'Don't let her eat the bloody thing!'

He took hold of her lead and pulled on it. The dog held on to the rabbit and growled at him.

Ruby grinned, still panting. 'You're never going to get that off her.'

'You try and grab it.'

He was facing the dog, pulling her towards him. The collar had ridden up on her neck and was stuck behind her ears. Her head was down low, close to the ground. She growled again.

'D'you think I'm mad?'

'Come and take the lead then.'

She obliged him. He moved closer to the dog, circling her, bent down slowly and then lunged at the rabbit. She snarled, still holding on, and jumped forwards, towards Ruby, altering Ruby's centre of gravity and toppling her over. As she fell she let go of the lead. The dog dashed away, carrying the rabbit with her.

'Are you all right?'

She sat up, slightly winded, and tried to dust herself off. He offered her his hand. Her first impulse was to spit on it, but she reached out and took hold of it.

Ruby apologized for being late, and was about to explain about the state of her clothes when the area manager, Tom Croft, emerged from the kitchen carrying a bundle of notes through from the safe. He had yellow hair and a long, soft chin.

'So you finally made it?'

'I just told Jason . . .'

'What are you wearing?'

She said nothing. He stared at her coolly. 'You think this job is so difficult? There are plenty of others who could manage to do it, come in on time and dress properly.'

He pointed towards the till closest to where she was standing. 'I suggest you get some work done.'

Ruby sat down at the till and was about to give it a routine check when a punter came up for a bet. She rang it on, took the money and thanked him. When he'd gone, she took out the larger notes and counted them.

'Jason, this is a tenner short. Did you put in a float this morning?'

Jason was about to say something when Croft interrupted: 'I've been using that till myself all morning. It was fine when you sat down there two minutes ago.'

'Well, it's not fine now and I've only taken one small bet.'

'Are you sure that's all you've taken?'

'What?'

She noticed that Jason was blushing. Croft said, 'You've signed on. You should've checked the till first. The loss of that money is now your responsibility.'

He pulled on his jacket. 'I want you properly dressed next time I see you and I want you in on time.'

He strolled out.

As soon as he was gone she turned on Jason. 'I don't believe this! He practically called me a thief.'

'At least he didn't give you a formal warning.'

'That isn't the point. Where's Dawn?'

'I dunno. Not here yet.'

'If I'd been ten minutes later, I'd have missed him too.'

Jason smiled grimly. 'Knowing your luck, he'd have waited.'

'Oh yeah?'

She pulled off her sweatshirt and sat down. 'What bloody luck?'

Already Sarah could smell something strange. Her olfactory senses were incredibly refined. Her gut was stimulated not so much by sight as by sound and by smell. It churned as this new, unexpected aroma entered her nostrils and gained access to her interior. When she inhaled a good or a bad smell she sometimes felt as though she were actually eating it. Aromas were like foods but were less physically complex, like a kind of dispersed matter. When she inhaled them they invaded her, filled her and travelled through her system.

She tried to think of something else. 'What's your mother called again?'

'Brera.'

'Weird name.'

'It's Irish.'

'Nice name.'

'Yeah.'

'Don't the lifts work?'

'There aren't any. It's only five floors.'

By the fifth floor, Sarah was breathing so heavily that she couldn't smell anything.

Sam opened the door and ushered Sarah inside. It was dark. They walked down the passageway and into the living-room. Sam was about to switch on the light, but then resisted and strolled over towards the window instead, intending to draw the curtains. She bumped into an armchair. The furniture had been moved around. She grabbed hold of a curtain and was just about to yank it open when she heard Brera's voice.

'Leave those.'

She paused.

'Don't open the curtains. Sylvia's on the sofa. She's had a bad attack.'

Sam squinted around her in the half-light. 'Well, she's not there now.'

'Damn!'

Brera turned and headed towards Sylvia's bedroom. Earlier she had taken the precaution of locking the door. She tried the handle. It was still locked. She peered into Sam's bedroom but this room was also empty. She turned towards the bathroom. She tried the door but the bolt inside had been shot across.

'Sylvia?'

No reply.

'The window's jammed in there. You won't get it open.'

She heard a quiet, scraping noise, like the sound of soft sandpaper against wood. Then she realized that this was actually Sylvia's voice.

'I know that.'

'Come out, then.'

'Later.'

She could hear the gentle wheezing of Sylvia's breath.

'What're you doing?'

Sylvia's voice was raw but censorious. 'I'm having a crap, all right?'

Brera scowled and turned to see Sam and Sarah, standing directly behind her. Sarah was smirking.

'Who's this?'

'Sarah.'

Brera felt ridiculous.

In the kitchen, she filled the kettle, plugged it in and turned it on. 'She nearly died yesterday.'

This was her excuse.

Sam sat down but said nothing. This irritated Brera, who could still visualize the horror of the day before: Sylvia's blotchy face and clenched teeth, the *sounds* she made.

Sarah was leaning against the door, one hand on the handle, pushing it up and down. After a while Sam said, 'She seems fine now.'

Brera dropped her voice: 'Not really. She can hardly walk. Hardly breathe. I decided it'd be best if we cancelled the photographer. That was all sorted and then Steven phoned last night . . .'

'Why are you whispering?'

Brera put a finger to her lips. 'He phoned last night and said he'd managed to organize a small club tour. Only about ten dates, but it starts almost immediately. Some singer dropped out at the last minute. Irish pubs and clubs. Mainly in the north.'

They all turned as they heard the toilet flush, and, after a short duration, the slow sound of the bathroom door being unbolted.

Sylvia staggered back to the living-room. It took her several minutes. She sat down on the sofa and tried to calm herself. She felt terrible, but this sick feeling, this illness, was paradoxically reassuring. It was simpler than everything else. There was something intimate and familiar about it. She smiled to herself and thought, Sickness is like a boyfriend.

She stopped smiling and frowned. That morning she had awoken and her mind had been full of one thing, one word. The word was *virus*. She couldn't stop thinking about it. Virus! The idea of it had stuck with her. She thought, Life is about man battling with the virus. The virus is like a force, but something so simple, so destructive. And man, in all his complexity, can't beat it. He can't beat the virus.

The thought of this made her skin crawl, but it made her feel gratified too and strangely calm.

Ruby's bad start had infected her entire day. She'd argued with several customers, had broken the printing mechanism on her till before the biggest race of the afternoon, had spilled tea over one of Dawn's magazines and had dropped the sugar bowl on the floor in the kitchen.

As she climbed the stairs up to her flat, the sugar on the soles of her trainers made an irritating gritty noise against the linoleum.

Almost at the landing, she met a neighbour: a small, mousy-haired girl who wore John Lennon glasses and baggy trousers. She was on her way down. She stopped Ruby as she moved past her, taking hold of the sleeve of her sweatshirt: 'Ruby, is there an animal of some kind in your flat?'

Ruby almost smiled. Vincent, she thought, but said, 'A dog.'

'Terry was sniffing around earlier. You'd best get rid of it.'

Terry was the caretaker.

'Hell. That's all I need.'

She took out her keys and unlocked the door to her flat. She could hear music inside. She couldn't place it, though. As she opened the door she listened more attentively.

Vincent was standing in the kitchen wielding a large bread knife.

'What're you doing?'

She walked over to the stereo and turned the volume down.

'Dinner.' He grinned at her. 'Watch this.'

He bent down low, disappearing from sight behind the work surface. After several seconds he raised his arm, bringing his right hand into view. On it, cleverly reassembled in macabre puppet form, was the tattered rabbit skin. He bounced it along the counter, waving the rabbit's paws and nodding its head.

Ruby covered her mouth with her hand. 'That's disgusting.'

The rabbit clapped its paws and then bowed.

She felt queasy. 'Get rid of it. It's horrible.'

Vincent stood up, the rabbit still covering his hand, and strolled towards her.

She took a step backwards. 'Keep it away from me.'

She moved behind the armchair.

'For God's sake, it's only a piece of fur.'

She tried to distract him. 'Where's the dog?'

'The rabbit ate her.'

He moved around the armchair. Ruby continued to back away. 'Is she in the bedroom?'

'Might be.'

'Something's burning.'

'Onions. They aren't burning.'

Ruby stepped up against the sofa and then toppled on to it. Vincent bent over towards her, holding the rabbit only inches from her face and clapping its paws together as if intending to grab hold of her nose. She yelled and tried to escape sideways, but Vincent was too quick for her. He grabbed her arm with his free hand and pushed her flat on to the sofa. She struggled, but he held her hips down with his knee and moved his free hand to her shoulder.

'Get lost!'

Her face was scarlet. She was perfectly serious. Vincent was laughing.

He said, 'I won't put it in your face, honestly.'

Instead he pulled up her sweatshirt and stuck the rabbit between her breasts. This time Ruby screamed. She pushed Vincent's hand and knee away and ripped at her sweatshirt. Vincent rolled off her and on to the floor, roaring.

Ruby could feel the sticky fur and skin of the rabbit against her bare flesh, but she couldn't bear to pull it out with her hands. Instead she pulled off her sweatshirt and watched disgustedly as the rabbit fell to the floor. Vincent put out his arm to reach for it, but she kicked it away and then kicked him in the stomach.

'Fuck!'

He grabbed her foot and twisted it, bringing her down heavily

114

on top of him. He was winded but still gasping with laughter. Ruby tried to scramble to her feet, but he stuck one of her arms behind her back and held it painfully in this position.

Her face was pressed into his shoulder. She bit him in the soft flesh between his shoulder-blade and his armpit. He swore and then tossed her over on to her back and straddled her stomach.

At this point it dawned on him that she was wearing no shirt, only a black bra. Her pale skin underneath it felt like candle wax.

She said, 'I could really hurt you if I chose to, but I choose not to.'

He laughed. 'You think so?'

He touched the place where she had bitten him. 'I bet you pierced the skin.'

She stared at his hand. It was caked with dry blood from the rabbit. He looked at it and smiled. 'Rabbit blood.'

She wondered whether he intended to lean over and kiss her. She thought, It'd take so little effort to kiss me now. He will kiss me.

But he didn't. He put his hands on the floor, either side of her, and pushed himself up. She thought, He doesn't even want to.

She lifted her foot and kicked him squarely between the thighs.

He yelled. His legs buckled and his expression lost all traces of merriment. She scrambled to her feet, pushed him over sideways and used all her weight and strength to hold him down.

His face was pale. She smiled dryly to herself, pinning his arms to the floor with her knees.

Gradually he regained some of his colour. She leaned over him. He opened his eyes and looked into her face. She stared back at him, still holding him down firmly, although he offered no opposition. She moved slowly and deliberately closer to his face and then kissed his nose, his lips. These were small kisses, soft kisses, her lips puckered loosely as though she were about to suck a lychee.

He turned his head away. 'Don't do that. Don't touch me.'

She pulled back.

'Where's the dog?'

'In the bedroom.'

'Right.'

She stood up and looked around for her sweatshirt. It was slung over the arm of the sofa. She grabbed it and held it to her chest as she walked over to her bedroom. Opening the door, she said, 'Those onions still smell like they're burning.'

He sat up. 'How was work?'

'I had a terrible day.'

She went into her room. 'And I've got to go out now.'

'Where?'

He scrambled to his feet and went into the kitchen.

'To take some photos. I won't have time to eat.'

'It'll keep.'

Scowling, he turned off the oven.

Ruby closed her bedroom door and leaned up against it. She felt sick.

The dog was stretched out on her bed. She opened a lazy eye and perused Ruby with it. Her tail thumped gently against the pillow. Ruby walked to her cupboard and searched for something special to wear. She wanted to look good. She had been insulted.

At the back of her wardrobe was a cotton dress, plainly cut, flattering but not too short. She took it out and inspected it. It was black with a thin white band around the neck and hem.

She pulled it over her head and put her arms through the armholes, but before she pulled it down, she yanked off her trainers and stepped out of her jeans, spat on her hand and rubbed it between her breasts to eliminate any final traces of the rabbit, then adjusted the dress and looked around for a pair of sheer black tights. She found some, checked them for holes and then sat down on the bed to pull them on. As she eased them over her feet and stretched them up her calves she thought, Does he hate me now? Does he think I'm easy?

She hated that word.

Did she like him? She remembered Sunday and the incident with Donald Sheldon. On Sunday I convinced myself that I liked Don Sheldon and I've never fancied him.

She stood up and pulled the tights over her bottom and thighs, settling the elastic comfortably around her waist. Would I have had sex with Vincent? Yes? What did he mean, 'Don't touch me'? What does that mean?

Shoes.

She searched for a specific pair of high-heeled black shoes. She found them under her bed and slipped them on, then stared down at her feet and thought, How can I fancy him?

All she could think of was that moment, on Saturday, when she had walked into the burger bar and he had been standing by the counter. It was a random moment, but the thought of it seemed to satisfy her in some way – nothing specific about the moment, but the moment itself.

She liked his carelessness.

She marched to the door and opened it. Vincent was leaning against the oven. He hadn't moved. He stared at her. She felt her insides swelling.

'What's up?' He asked this aggressively, defensively.

She glared at him, not understanding what he meant. She said, 'I'm in a hurry.'

She turned and went into the bathroom, inspected her face in the mirror and picked up her make-up bag.

Vincent called through from outside, 'I'll get the dog ready.'

'Why?'

'We'll come too.'

She didn't want him to come, but said, 'The camera stuff is under my bed, in a black case. It's all there. Get the dog muzzled.'

He popped his head around the bathroom door. 'I like that dress.'

'You're welcome to borrow it.'

She turned back to the mirror and reapplied her lipstick. She thought, *Don't touch me*? Jesus.

Sam walked through to the living-room. It was dark and stuffy in here. She perched on the arm of the sofa, inspected the nebulizer and then the top of Sylvia's head, which was all but covered by a blanket. She could hear her breathing rattling underneath it.

'You must be boiling under there.'

Sylvia moved slightly.

'Sounds like you had a bad attack yesterday.'

No movement.

'Mum was telling me how you went out on Saturday night and that you've been strange ever since.'

Sylvia's body stiffened. Sam noticed. That's odd, she thought.

'Was someone rude to you?'

Sylvia pulled the blanket away from her face. 'Who's that girl?'

'Sarah? She's a nurse. She's going to look after you while Mum and I go away for a few days.'

'She's no nurse.'

'No, she's just a friend.'

'You're going away, though.'

'We've been offered a small tour, but Mum isn't keen to leave you, especially now you're so sick.'

Sylvia tucked the blanket more tightly around her chin.

Sam changed tack. 'Your breathing sounds terrible, like the noise a balloon makes when you let go of it and the air speeds out. Like a whistle. Have you tried the nebulizer?'

'Last night. A bit this morning.'

'You'll be on steroids again if you're not careful.'

'I won't be.'

Sam paused for a moment and then said, 'What about your room?'

Sylvia turned, suddenly attentive. 'Can you get the key?'

'I don't know. Maybe.'

'How?'

'If you act reasonably over this tour thing, I'll try and talk her round. Otherwise . . .' She made an expansive gesture with her hands. 'She might have you locked out here for good.'

Sylvia started to say something but the entry-phone buzzed. Sam stood up. 'That'll be Sarah. She just popped out to get some wine. I could bring you a glass if you like.'

Sylvia grimaced, turned over and pressed her face into the

118

back of the sofa. 'I don't want anything. Keep her away from me.'

Her throat tightened.

'I'm not being rude,' Sarah said, sipping from her glass, comfortably ensconced at the end of the table, 'but in performance terms, in any terms, it probably wouldn't occur to most people that the two of you were even related.'

Brera was infuriated by this.

'We are though,' Sam said.

Brera added, 'In a way that makes it even better. More dramatic.'

Brera didn't actually know what she was talking about. This was Sam's concern. Even so, Sarah gave her comment some consideration. 'Well, it adds another dimension, certainly.'

Sam realized – and it came almost as a shock – that she didn't like justifying herself, only explaining, only . . . not even discussing. Just talking.

She didn't want to think about being different. They were all women, after all. That united them. Colour separated her from Brera, from Sylvia, but *gender*, that was what connected them. They understood each other. Their breasts, their vaginas. Sarah too. They were all the same.

Sylvia was escaping. Had to. Get some air. She made it to the door. The front door. They hadn't locked it. Sarah's fault. She pulled it open and stared into the hallway.

Two people were there, on the doorstep, engaged in an argument. They stopped when they saw her. She was wearing only a T-shirt, knickers and socks. Her mask was attached to her nose and mouth, but the wire dangled, unplugged, across her shoulder.

Two people and a dog.

Vincent had just told Ruby about Steven's phone call. Ruby focused on Sylvia and began to say something, Sylvia simply turned her back on them, hopeless now, and started her journey back inside. She put her hand out to the wall to steady herself –

everything achingly slow – and found instead Ruby beside her, Ruby's hand steadying her, Ruby's arm and Ruby's shoulder.

Sylvia caught hold of Ruby's hand. 'What's that?'

Ruby could barely understand her growl, but said, 'It's a bird.'

'What does it mean?'

'I did it years ago.'

They shuffled inside. Vincent followed, like a porter, he thought, with the dog and the case.

Sylvia maintained her tight grip on Ruby. No one understood her here. She had to find understanding.

'Shall I put the light on?' Vincent asked in the hallway, and then, on receiving no reply, in the living-room.

Ruby settled Sylvia on the sofa. 'Best leave it off.'

Sylvia's breathing sounded like the noise a young fledgling might make, a mouse.

'You can't be either Sam or Brera.'

Vincent inspected the nebulizer. Sylvia indicated the refill bottle with her foot. He picked it up and tipped some inside where she showed him. She turned it on.

'Why are you doing that?' Ruby asked, suspicious.

'Air conditioning,' Vincent said. The smell in the flat was sickening.

Sylvia started to tell them both about the virus, still wearing her mask. Ruby sat down with her. Vincent squatted next to Ruby, closest to the machine and its expulsions.

'Several . . . jangles . . . body-part . . . layer . . . transaction . . . locomotive . . .'

They couldn't understand her. The nebulizer was steaming, producing a vapour, a heady, menthol mix. Their eyes began to stream. They were sniffing, inhaling something spectacular, the weirdest potion. After a while they were all laughing for no particular reason. Ruby was sure that she felt Vincent touching her leg, her tights, feeling her shoes. Was he really doing that? The air was so warm, so warm, and something else . . . Why was she here? She couldn't focus. She struggled to remember.

*

Sam was on her third glass of wine. Sarah was discussing a trip she'd taken to the Philippines when she was eighteen. Brera felt something soft and moist against her thigh. Wine usually made her feel this way, but inside her chest, her stomach . . .

Sam, opposite Brera, sensed something vibrating between her knees. Their eyes met. 'I think it's a dog,' Brera said, bursting out laughing. They peered under the table.

'Where on earth did you come from?'

Sam listened intently for a moment and thought that she heard mutterings from elsewhere in the flat: chanting, grunting, stifled guffaws.

In the living-room, the darkness, she found them. The atmosphere had overloaded with the scent of ripe menthol.

'How long have you all been here?'

She tried to open the door on to the roof, but of course it was locked. Instead she opened the curtains and the window.

'You must be Sam . . . or Brera.' Ruby tried to stand up. Failed.

'What are you all doing?'

'I'm supposed to be taking some photographs. Steven sent me.'

Sam walked over and switched off the nebulizer. She waved her arms around, trying to improve the circulation of air. 'It's like an opium den in here. That stuff's toxic if it isn't used properly.'

She noticed that Sylvia was holding Ruby's hand and that her mask was unplugged.

If this girl, Sylvia thought, tells Sam I was trying to escape . . .

'We knocked on the door and your friend answered,' Ruby said.

'My sister.'

This was a mistake everyone made.

Sylvia grinned, under her mask, victorious.

'I only just found out we weren't even supposed to come,' Ruby added, apologetically, 'which is a pity, really, because the light's brilliant.'

She squinted towards the window. Samantha, her back to the sun, glowed with an almost supernatural beauty.

'Are you all OK?' Sam asked, staring at the three of them. They seemed in a state of collapse, appeared limp and giggly.

Ruby pulled herself up straight. 'I feel a bit dizzy.'

'You're always doing this,' Sam said, directly to Sylvia, 'using something good and getting the worst out of it.'

'What does that mean?' Vincent wondered out loud, speaking for the first time, his voice slow and his face groggy.

Sarah strolled in with the dog trailing behind her. Vincent slapped his thigh and Buttercup trotted over. Sarah smiled at him. 'Is it yours?'

'She,' he said, with great deliberation, 'is a bitch.'

Sam said, 'If the light's so good, then maybe we should do the pictures after all.'

She didn't want to waste this opportunity. Ruby looked down, still dazed, and noticed that her dress was all rucked up. She tried to smooth it straight.

'Are you a photographer?' Sarah asked Vincent, focusing on the cut across his forehead.

'I'm her assistant.'

'What does an assistant do?'

'Assist.'

'Come with me,' Sam said. 'We can find Brera and see what she thinks.'

Ruby let go of Sylvia's hand. Sylvia's eyes filled with tears. Sam noticed. 'What's wrong?'

'The light, that's all.'

Sarah and Vincent were still talking. Sam closed the window and drew the curtains again.

In Sam's bedroom, clothes were strewn across the bed. 'Something plain is probably best,' Ruby said.

Sam felt irritable, but she wasn't sure why. It wasn't clothes. Nothing cosmetic.

'My sister really took a shine to you.'

'She liked the tattoo on my hand. She wouldn't let go of me after she'd seen it.'

Like something I saw in a dream, Ruby thought, that girl, this smell, this feeling.

She couldn't stop staring at Sam. She was like an angel. 'You'd look good in anything,' she said. 'A bin-bag with a piece of string as a belt.'

Sam smiled as she pulled on a plain white shirt and a black skirt.

'Where have you come from?'

'Soho.'

'A studio?'

'I live there.'

'Sounds glamorous.'

Ruby laughed. 'Hardly. I like it here better. It's near to the track where I race my dog.'

Sam could hear Sarah laughing in the kitchen. She felt disgruntled, but she wasn't sure why. She picked up some eye-liner and applied it carefully.

'Well, the light's still fantastic,' Ruby said, trying to sound like she knew what this meant. Brera and Sam both held their guitars under their arms like machine guns. Ruby couldn't be bothered with the tripod. She took out her camera and tried to focus it.

'Sing something.'

They began to strum 'Jesus Don't Want Me for a Sunbeam'. Connor had taught them this tune on Sunday.

Ruby felt tipsy. Was the film in? Did she need a flash? The air, at least, was clearer out here. She inhaled deeply and then started to shoot.

She had no particular talent for photography. She worked on the premise that the more film she used, the more likely it would be that a clutch of snaps would turn out decently. Brera wore a long, grey, smock-like dress, her red hair loose. Ruby focused on her. It was easy. They did a song by Captain Beefheart.

Where was Vincent? She didn't care. But where was he?

Sam said, 'I've half a mind to call Sarah out. She mentioned earlier that she'd like to hear us.'

Brera began playing again. This time, a strange song, a song without a middle, an end, a chorus. Ruby was dazed by it. She was still frizzy. Her mouth – inside – felt gluey and sticky. The song started up, flew off and didn't come back. Like modern art, she thought. She'd never been able to understand that either.

After they'd finished, Sam said, 'Sylvia wrote it.'

Sarah popped her head out, around the door, and shaded her eyes against the sunlight. 'I could hear you all the way through in the kitchen just then,' she said. 'I thought it was a cat fight.'

'Things can still be interesting,' Ruby interjected quickly, 'even if you don't understand them.'

Sam started playing something else. Sarah stepped outside and lounged against the brickwork.

Inside, Sylvia prepared a mental salad with all the voices in the flat. Sarah, she decided, was a radish. A small, round, purple thing; fibrous. She took out a sharp knife and sliced Sarah in half and then into quarters. She poked the knife into her again and again and again. Until, eventually, she was only pulp.

Back in the kitchen, Brera volunteered to make Ruby some coffee. Ruby sat at the table, putting film into containers, removing lenses and packing things away. The others were still outside. Vincent had been helping himself to the wine and had become, unexpectedly, positively garrulous.

'You must have photographed lots of people,' Brera said, smiling.

'Some.'

'It wasn't too formal, which was great.'

The dog trotted in and sat down next to Ruby. Ruby stroked her. Brera leaned against the sink. 'Sam said she'd never seen Sylvia so friendly with a stranger before. She's not generally so tactile.'

'She seems very weak.'

'She's ill.'

'I like her.'

'Where do you live?'

'Sam asked me that. In Soho. In a flat. It's much smaller than this.'

'Is it nice?'

Ruby shrugged and continued stroking.

'Does Steven pay you much for taking pictures?'

'If he likes them. I hope he will. I need the money.'

'Sam said you raced the dog.'

'At Hackney Wick. Just down the road.'

'Do you like this flat?'

Ruby frowned. 'It's nice.'

'The dog likes it.'

Brera, Ruby decided, was barking mad.

'You must think I'm mad,' Brera said, pulling out a chair and sitting down. 'I'm not mad, but I've just had a mad idea.'

That's how it starts, though, Ruby thought. Mad ideas, doing mad things, *being* mad.

In the pub, facing an interviewer, a small tape recorder and a bottle of Newcastle Brown, Connor had felt the need to blow his nose. He put his hand in his pocket to pull out a handkerchief but instead, accidentally, pulled out Sam's brassière.

Small, white, soft.

This, he thought, is a real rock cliché.

Afterwards, though, whenever he spoke, whatever he said, he could think only of Sam. His mind was full of her. Where she was going. What she was doing.

Brera's idea was that Ruby should move into Jubilee Road with the dog for an initial period of two weeks while the Goldhawk Girls went on tour. Brera assured her that she would keep in constant contact and that Ruby would receive a percentage of their earnings for her services. Sam strolled in to get a clean glass and Brera filled her in. She was enthusiastic. She said, 'We could give you twenty-five per cent. Sylvia would have to get her cut too. It should end up being a reasonable amount.'

Ruby agreed that the money would be useful. 'But the problem is . . .' She cleared her throat. 'The real problem is that you don't even know me and I don't even know Sylvia.'

Brera shrugged. 'I think we could trust you. Sylvia's an adult. She doesn't need constant attention.'

Ruby felt as though Sam and Brera presumed some kind of

awareness on her part about Sylvia's particular circumstances, but in fact she couldn't make any sense at all of the situation. Her brain was swamped with images – her own inky, blue tattoo; a retchingly acrid smell that pervaded every corner of the flat; Sylvia herself, white, acerbic, wheezing; the dark rooms; the nebulizer.

'I don't know.'

'We're near the track,' Sam offered helpfully.

'True.'

She didn't know whether to tell them that she worked full-time, just in case Steven had told them something himself that she'd be obliged to contradict. Eventually she said, 'How about you discuss this with Steven first?'

Brera nodded. 'We'd have to ask him for some kind of reference.'

They were still in the kitchen, three of them now, sitting around the table. Ruby stood up and placed her mug in the sink. 'You could get Steven to ring me later. You could mention the idea to Sylvia as well and see how she reacts.'

Vincent came in, holding the dog by her collar. 'I just took her out for a pee.'

'We're going now, anyway.'

Sam stood up too. 'Where's Sarah?'

He grabbed the dog's lead. 'I heard her talking to your sister.'

Sam had been smiling, but her smile disappeared. She was starting to wish she'd kept Sarah all to herself. Connor, it turned out, could be right about some things.

Sarah pulled up a chair next to the sofa. Sylvia was under her blanket.

'Hi. I'm Sarah, Sam's friend. We haven't been properly introduced yet. I saw you earlier.'

Sylvia didn't reply.

'I heard you chatting to Vincent just now.'

Nothing.

Sarah thought Sylvia was just like a child. If you wanted her to do something, she wouldn't do it. She was simply contrary. This

126

was her way of asserting herself. She wouldn't conform. She was outside things. Sarah understood this, wanted to let Sylvia know that she understood. She started talking. And she talked.

'I read *The Female Eunuch* years ago, and when I got to the part about feeling pride in your own femininity, I discovered something very disturbing about myself.'

Silence.

'Greer said that if you aren't ashamed of being a woman, then it should be possible to dip your finger into your vagina, during your period, to immerse your finger in menstrual blood and then to put that finger into your mouth without any feelings of disgust.'

Nothing.

'I tried it. I tried it, but I just couldn't do it. I tried for years, every month, and each time I failed I felt so bloody guilty.'

Sylvia shifted under the blanket. Sarah noticed and took this to be a positive sign.

'Then it dawned on me that the only reason I felt disgusted was because of a natural fastidiousness. I suddenly thought, How the hell does Greer get off on telling me how to feel about my sense of self? I know how I feel.'

Under the blanket Sylvia put a furtive hand between her legs.

'Setting tests is a kind of masculine construct. If something doesn't come naturally, then, quite simply, it isn't natural.'

Sylvia drew back her blankets and, in the darkness, held something aloft between her finger and thumb. Sarah squinted through the half-light and saw that Sylvia was holding a used tampon, dangling it by its string as though it were a small, live mouse.

Sarah felt her gorge rise. Sylvia stuck the tampon between her teeth – like a short, fat, pink cheroot – closed her lips and sucked.

Sarah could hear the cotton wool squeaking against her teeth.

Ruby was locked in her bathroom, bathed in a red light, developing the photographs. Outside she could hear Vincent clattering around.

They'd begun arguing on the bus during the ride home. She'd

made the mistake of mentioning Brera's scheme to him. She hadn't thought it would prove all that contentious. It wasn't as though he even appeared to have any kind of objection to the scheme itself. At one point, though, when she'd said, 'Maybe one day I'll get to rent a proper house with a garden and all that stuff,' he'd said, 'You're a shithead.'

'Thanks.'

Vincent and the dog were on the sofa together, watching television, when Ruby finally emerged from the bathroom, smelling of chemicals.

'D'you want to see the pictures?'

He put out his hand. She passed one copy of each of the prints to him.

Something smelled good in the kitchen. She walked over and peered into a pan on the stove. 'What's this?'

'It's probably ruined by now.'

'Can I have some?'

Vincent held up one of the prints. 'I've been thinking about money.'

'What?' She had expected a comment on the quality of her work.

'I said . . .' He perused the print as he held it aloft. 'Brera's eyes are skew.'

'Are they?'

Ruby walked across and peered at the photo over his shoulder. 'It's just that she's singing and focusing on the camera at the same time. Sam looks fantastic. Those lashes.'

'She's like a racehorse.'

'How's that?'

'A painting in the National Gallery.'

She grinned. 'Very poetic.'

He handed back the pictures. She slid them carefully into an envelope.

'You could make some money you know, get the money you need for the dog, and you wouldn't even have to do anything.'

'Oh yeah?'

'Sit down.'

She sat on the sofa, pushing the dog's legs over, lifting them and arranging them across her lap.

'Shall I give you some advice?'

Blue, blue eyes, he had. She frowned. 'Is it sensible to take advice from someone who doesn't give a damn about anything?'

'Yes, if it's good advice.'

And the funny thing is, she thought, I know exactly what kind of advice it will be.

The dog's nose was touching his thigh. This meant that the two of them were touching, were linked, indirectly.

'You handle a fortune every day. And if you think about it, it isn't even as though the money belongs anywhere.'

'It doesn't belong to me, that's for sure.'

'You owe a fair amount.'

She knew this. And that he owed her.

'You are owed,' he said, with great certainty.

'So what?'

'Listen to me.' He leaned closer. 'Between the two of us we could make money without actually even taking anything.'

She was so tired, all of a sudden.

He outlined his plan.

'No.'

'Why not?'

'It's stupid.'

'It's not stupid.'

'No.'

He had rejected her, that afternoon, in this very room. She would deny him whatever she could. For any reason. She would deny him.

THIRTEEN

Sylvia stood by the window. The curtains closed behind her.

Where do thoughts go? she wondered. They travel, in your voice, out of your body, in waves, into other people's ears. She breathed on the glass. Where do they start? A circuit connecting? With an electric buzz? A chemical reaction?

She pushed at the glass. Still weak. It wouldn't open. Sam had opened it, the day before, effortlessly. Would she smash it? She thought that she might, she considered doing it, but she didn't.

A small bird on a telephone wire. Something travelled through his feet. He vibrated. She filled him with her thoughts, and his body contained, so perfectly, the contents of her mind.

Off he flew.

He saw things. He saw the city from above and from below. He saw trees, small, like pieces of broccoli; a blade of grass, big as, bigger than, himself. A worm, on concrete. It would curl up in his stomach.

He saw many things, and many of the things he saw meant nothing: a succession of images, only registered in his tiny brain, photographed but not digested.

Each day – she saw it clearly now – so little could happen. Each day, each person, every person, yearning for only one thing. To own, to love, to keep, to do, to forget, to try.

In Soho. Do it. I will not. Do it. I will not. A pattern, like the beat of a clock, a heart. Tick *tick*, tick *tick*, tick *tick*, tick *tick*.

Sam's mind, full of Sarah. Connor's mind, full of Sam. Brera's mind, full of Sylvia. Sylvia's mind, contained so easily, flying above the city.

FOURTEEN

What the hell had happened? A day of nagging, an ugly, pointless, driven, aimless time. He didn't want to think about it. Solid things. That was better. Something solid. Thursday. Yes. Bateman Street. Yes. Ladbrokes.

He was sitting on a small, red plastic stool. He was watching the television screen. How was he feeling? Defeated? Frustrated? There was no answer to that. He wouldn't provide an answer.

Ruby. She had refused him. He worried that she lacked understanding, and therefore, as a consequence, that she also lacked imagination. She's deceptive, he thought. She looks like she doesn't care, she lives like she doesn't care, but she does care. She does. He couldn't deny that he liked her strength, but her goodness?

On the screen appeared a list of the runners for the two o'clock at Hackney.

Was it goodness or was it just stupidity? No, not stupidity, worse than that. Conservatism.

He had wanted to go to the track with her, but he wouldn't admit it. He had been forced to argue with her instead, which, everything considered, was for the best.

He had been hoping for an outside trap for Buttercup: four, five or even six, but he saw immediately that she had been drawn in trap three. He felt around in his pockets and pulled out a handful of notes. He stared at the list of runners, trying to understand the odds. Buttercup was out at twenty-five to one. The favourite, a bitch called Karen's Special, was the four-to-five odds-on favourite. The commentator for the race was saying how she'd been dropped a grade because she'd just come out of season, so she was running well below her class. She was usually a railer, but was drawn in trap four.

'Right.'

The notes he was clutching had been removed that morning from Ruby's coffee jar. This was his revenge. He reached for a pen and was still scribbling on his slip when the commentator introduced a visual survey of the animals in the race. Six small figures led six tiny dogs in coloured jackets out on to the track. He saw Ruby immediately, saw, even from this great distance, that her jacket was ill-fitting – too large, greyish – and that her hair shone out like a clump of flossy white cotton. He found himself grinning.

He watched intently as each dog was paraded in front of the camera. Ruby was third. Her expression was serious as she posed Buttercup and encouraged her to stand straight, side-on, to her best advantage. The dog's tail, Vincent was pleased to note, wagged cheerily. Ruby did not look at her best on screen. In fact she looked rough – her expression tired, almost grim, and her face heavily made-up, especially her eyes, which looked too dark somehow, too hooded.

Vincent peered around him at the other punters. Most of them were staring into space, writing on their slips or inspecting their papers. He felt a tightness in his chest. This isn't sex, he told himself, refusing to even consider the word *affection*; not sex, only excitement.

Ruby had moved on and the favourite was now showing: a lean, slight, brindle bitch.

He picked up a pen and completed his slip. Trap four. A practical choice, a sensible gamble, free of sentiment. He visited the counter and returned to his stool.

On the screen the dogs were being loaded. Ruby, he noticed, was chatting to the person handling the dog next to her and smiling. What was she saying? Did she think she'd win? What was she thinking?

He listened to the whistle of the mechanical hare.

'Hello.'

Toro stood beside him, eating a doughnut.

'Hang on.'

The hare whizzed past the traps and at that same instant the

132

traps opened. Vincent's eyes were glued to the third trap. Buttercup sprang out.

'Yes!'

She shot out of the trap like a bullet and veered immediately towards the hare, smashing full-on into the dog to her right. This dog (the favourite) rolled twice and pushed into the dog from the fifth trap who had come out more slowly. Buttercup stumbled, found her feet and ran on, but was then cut out of the picture as the camera followed and focused on the leading dogs from traps one, two and six, who had come out unhindered.

Vincent jerked his head sideways as though endeavouring to see beyond the screen, beyond what the camera would show.

Traps one and two were running close to the rails, six was in the picture but running wide. By the third bend, six had fallen back and Buttercup had inched her way into view, running in enormous, exhaustive bounds, on the outside, eventually running close to the six dog and then overtaking him.

'Yes!'

Vincent bounced up from his stool, forgetting about his bet, thinking only about Buttercup. 'Go on, you silly bitch!'

He was so intent on watching Buttercup's progress, her every move, her every stride, that he failed to notice as the number one dog ran across the finishing line, followed closely by trap two.

The race was over. The hare stopped.

He looked down at his slip. 'That was quick.'

Toro put out his hand for the slip, but Vincent screwed it up and threw it at one of the television screens.

'Forget it. Come on.' He took hold of Toro's arm. 'Let's get drunk.'

Stan bent over and ran his hands down the dog's back, her rump and hocks. 'Seems OK. We're in seven kinds of shit, though.'

Ruby was patting Buttercup, was so proud of her. The dog was still jerky, panting, trembling.

'Did one of the other dogs get hurt in the tumble?'

He shrugged. 'I dunno. That's not our main problem. Our problem is the racing manager. He'll have to explain why an obvious wide runner got drawn in trap three. It's his responsibility. The punters'll be fuming, and if it looks bad for him, then it looks bad for you.'

'But it's . . .'

'His fault. Yeah, but that won't make him feel any better. It's not as though he's had any indication from her previous form.'

'No.'

'He might scratch her.'

Ruby's jaw dropped. 'He can't do that. She came third.'

She towered above Stan. He was a withered four foot nine, hunched and red-nosed. She waited for him to say something. The dog was sitting down now, panting, her paws still hot.

'Don lost a lot of money recently.'

'What?'

'Gambling. He lost a load gambling, so he sold a good dog from the kennels, and unloaded this bitch on you.'

'Well, he can't have been that desperate. I haven't even paid him yet.'

'Exactly.'

He gazed down at the dog.

Connor was in his bedroom practising on his drums and keeping up a frenetic, repetitive, hardcore beat. He stopped for an instant, flipped a drumstick into the air, caught it, and then commenced with another song. He laughed out loud, relishing the noise he was making, the tension he was releasing.

Tension?

Am I tense? Just thinking about it made him stiffen up even further, although his arms kept on banging and tapping and whipping.

Am I tense?

He was desperate to communicate with Sam. She'd been out of contact for . . . he counted the hours in time with each beat . . . fifty-one, fifty-two, fifty-three, fifty-four hours. He continued drumming, noticing how his heart had started to pump in time. One, two, three, four. One, two, three, four. Too quick, too speedy, too swift. He was warm, not warm, hot, not hot, wet. His head was wet.

I want to stop drumming but I can't. It was too loud, too fast. Sarah will think . . . two, three, four. What would Sarah think? He didn't give a damn what Sarah thought.

He felt as though his heart was beating so rapidly now that it was actually faster than the drums: double-time. His head began to feel light, soft and airy.

Calm down, calm down, two, three, four.

Sarah flung open his bedroom door. She had knocked twice but he hadn't heard.

'Would you give it a rest for a while? My head's splitting.'

He stopped immediately, was almost grateful to her.

She glanced at his face. 'You look terrible. As white as a sheet.'

He said nothing. She disappeared. He sat still, stared at the drumsticks in his hands, debated whether to start up again, but couldn't face it. He was wound up like a watch. His palms were damp. He needed to unwind.

He stood up, stepped carefully away from the kit and walked into the living-room. Sarah was in her bedroom. He could hear her hairdrier. She can't listen, he thought. He picked up the phone.

Sylvia never answered the phone. She lay on the sofa as it rang. She didn't even bother considering who it could be. She didn't know anybody.

Brera and Sam were out shopping. Again. She stared around the dark room. So this is how it's going to be from now on? She smiled to herself.

The telephone continued to ring. She sucked her teeth.

Connor was so shocked when someone answered that he actually dropped the receiver. He picked it up in time to hear a voice say, 'No one rings for this long.'

'It's me, Connor.'

'Who?' She knew perfectly well who he was.

'I'm a friend of Sam's. Is she there?'

Sylvia put down the phone and walked to the bathroom. She washed her hands, noting how much her eczema had improved over the past couple of days. She returned to the living-room and sat down on the sofa. Connor's voice vibrated in tiny sound-waves through the air. Eventually she stood up and strolled back over.

'Look, I'm tired.'

'Where have you been?'

'Why?'

'I just wondered.'

Sylvia debated whether to answer this and then said, 'I'm locked in.'

'You are?'

'Yes.'

'Are you all right?'

She grinned to herself. 'Are you all right?'

'Why shouldn't I be?'

'Why shouldn't I be?'

Connor scowled. 'What are you doing?'

'What are you doing?'

'Look, this is silly.'

'Silly?' She smirked. 'Well, you're paying, stupid.'

'Will he be gone all night?' Ruby asked, feeling relieved, but also defeated.

Toro was drunk, leaning against Ruby's doorframe and emitting yeasty belches. He shrugged.

'Where is he?'

He shrugged.

'Fine.'

She slammed the door and then opened it again. 'Don't you have any idea?'

He shook his head.

'Didn't he even give you a message for me?'

'I gave it to you.'

Ruby watched as he turned and staggered downstairs, hanging on to the banister for support. She closed the door and sat

136

down on the sofa again. The dog was asleep in her bedroom, but the flat still felt empty.

'Bastard.' Her voice sounded ludicrously small.

She wanted a drink. A lager. She was peckish. A kebab. She stood up, went into the kitchen, opened the cupboard and took out her coffee jar. She took off the lid and peered inside. No money. What had he done with it?

She wasn't so much angry as hungry. She put down the jar and looked around for Vincent's rucksack. It was still on the floor next to the sofa. She frowned. Did I really think he'd gone? He wouldn't go like that.

She picked some mould off a piece of bread and put it in the toaster.

Two hours later they were still on the phone. Nothing real or significant, in conversational terms, had been achieved during this time. Connor had tried, on several occasions, to turn the subject of their conversation around to topics closer to his heart, but such attempts had proved futile. He said, 'About Sam . . .'

Sylvia cleared her throat and then cleared it again. Her throat never felt fully clear. After clearing her throat for a third time she said, 'My sister.'

'Yes.'

Connor hoped that Sylvia wouldn't go off at a tangent again. He was sick of the virus. She'd told him all about it. At inordinate length. Having a conversation with Sylvia was like blowing an egg. All the time you did it you could only think what a waste of energy it was, and sometimes the pin holes at either end would collapse and the overall effect would be entirely ruined.

Sylvia knew perfectly well that Connor only wanted to speak to her because he couldn't speak to Sam. She was obstructing him. It has also occurred to her that it was possible to do just about anything on the phone without the person at the other end having the slightest inkling. She considered some of the things that it would be possible to do and tried a few of them.

'About Sam . . .'

Sylvia didn't respond. She was inspecting the hair under her right arm while holding the phone slackly in her left.

'Is she busy at the moment?'

'How should I know?'

'Sarah told me . . .'

'Fuck her.'

'Who, Sarah?'

'Fuck her.'

'Sarah?'

'Fuck her.'

'I was told that Sam and Brera had several gigs lined up.' He'd tried to inject some enthusiasm into his voice.

'Ha!' Sylvia laughed and then coughed.

'What's so funny?'

She had just been sniffing the hair under her arm. She sniffed it again – deeply, fully – and inhaled the strong, pungent smell of old sweat. It was a horrible and yet a delicious smell.

Connor was still talking: 'I don't suppose you'd mind mentioning to her . . .'

Sylvia said, half to herself, 'Why did I put my nose there?'

'What?'

'Smell. I never noticed.'

'What?'

She stared around the room, looking for things that were aromatic. She put down the phone and muttered, 'If I didn't notice, maybe I couldn't. If I couldn't, then why did I put my nose under my arm?'

Connor sensed that all was not well at the other end. He could hear a selection of distant squawks and muffled thumps. He debated whether to hang up. Why am I speaking to this girl? Am I that fucked up over Sam?

On Tuesday when Sarah had returned home from Hackney she'd asked, 'Have you met Sylvia before?'

'Why?'

'Because she's a barbarian.'

'You don't like her?'

'She's like a big, brown, hairy man. She even speaks like a man.'

138

Connor had tried to imagine Sylvia as a man. He imagined Sam, but masculine. He liked the idea. Yet when he spoke to Sylvia, she didn't sound like a man at all, more like an old woman: stroppy, strained, dithering.

He wouldn't hang up. No. He held on.

Sylvia stood in the kitchen, staring into the fridge. She took out a bottle of milk and sniffed it.

'Oh my God!'

She shook her head, blinked, and then sniffed it again. 'Can I taste it? I can't taste it.'

She put it down, too frightened to try, reaching instead for a half-eaten packet of soft cheese. She pushed her face into it, covering the tip of her nose in its soft stickiness. She gasped, dropped the cheese, backed into the kitchen table, knocked over a chair and clutched at her face with both hands. She stood still, her two hands covering her nose, her breathing jerky and uncontrolled.

Connor was relieved when he heard her again.

'Hello?'

She was close to the phone, panting and hesitant. She picked up the receiver.

'Um.'

She was rubbing her nose with the flat of her palm. Her nose was now red from rubbing.

'What were you doing?'

'Nothing.'

Her response was too quick, he thought. He smiled to himself. 'You said something before . . . something about a smell.'

'I did?'

'Yes.'

'Um. Shit.'

'What?'

'Go away.'

'I heard you shouting.'

'I dropped something.'

'You know . . .' He paused for a moment. 'Today your voice sounds a whole lot better.'

She stopped rubbing her nose. She cleared her throat. It felt empty and unobstructed. She tried to clarify her thoughts, but couldn't.

'Look, don't tell anyone.'

Connor sounded thrilled: 'Don't tell them what?'

'About this. The smell. It's nothing. OK?'

'OK.'

'OK?'

'All right.'

'They're coming.'

She slammed down the phone and ran to the sofa, jumped on to it and pulled up her blanket.

'Oh no.'

It smelled awful. She took a gulp of air and then thrust her head under.

Connor listened to the dialling tone for a while and then hung up. He returned to his bedroom, closed the door and sat down on his bed. He thought, She's up to something, and, whatever it is, I'm sure Sam would appreciate knowing about it.

He lay down. She's up to something, but what the hell could it be? That girl, he decided, is a nut.

Steven was staring around the living-room. 'This place is disgusting.'

He had brought some wine. Ruby washed up a glass and a mug.

'Where's your friend?'

'Which friend?'

Steven kicked Vincent's rucksack. 'That friend.'

'Out.'

She didn't fancy explaining.

'The photos are on top of the speaker if you want to take a look.'

He picked up the envelope, opened it and sat down in the armchair. After inspecting three or four he said, 'These aren't too bad.'

She uncorked the wine, poured them both some, and then slouched across the sofa. She drained her mug in one gulp and gave herself some more. Steven opened his briefcase and slid the photos inside. 'I'll pay you later.'

'Fine.'

Ruby rolled on to her back and shut her eyes.

'Brera mentioned that you were considering staying in their flat while they do the gigs.'

'Did she?'

'You seem fed up.'

'Do I?'

'You are fed up.'

Steven cupped his wineglass between his large, pale hands. His hands dwarfed the glass. He looked like an enormous gnome handling a bubble.

'Well, if you're intending to do it, you should tell me. The first gig is on Saturday.'

He stared at her for a while. 'You seem disorganized.'

'I am.'

Ruby pulled herself up. 'Lately I feel like the top of my head's disappeared.'

His expression didn't change.

'I'm not being practical. It's my own fault.'

He opened his briefcase and took out the photos again.

'Do they really want me to stay in their flat?'

He looked up. 'I think they do. They don't seem very motivated, though. No one is, apart from me.'

'That's your job.'

'Well, if you do stay in Hackney, I'd have one less thing to worry about. I told them you were reliable.'

'What about the smell?'

'You'd get used to it quickly enough.'

'What about when I'm out at work?'

'She doesn't need nursing or guarding.'

'Brera said . . .'

'Brera's very protective, but Sylvia's independent.'

As he spoke, he remembered how she'd looked the other day when he'd picked her up and carried her to the door. How light she'd been.

*

141

'Sylvia's being weird.'

Sam whispered this to Brera. Brera was sitting at the kitchen table working out their finances. Sam was standing in the doorway holding a tray which held a cup of cold tea and an untouched meal.

'She wouldn't eat anything. When I asked why, she said she only wanted a glass of water.'

'Has she used her inhaler tonight?'

'I couldn't smell any vapour. I think she's up to something.'

'She's missing her birds.'

'Yeah, but it's more than that.'

'You think she's trying to stop us from going away?'

'Not necessarily. Earlier she asked when it was that we were going, as though she was actually looking forward to it.'

'Maybe she's planning to starve herself.'

'Possibly.' Sam didn't sound convinced.

'Maybe it's still to do with her trip out on Saturday. She's been strange ever since.'

'Couldn't you have a word with her?'

'She'd think I was prying.'

'Take her some water. Try and be subtle.'

Brera picked up a glass from the draining-board and ran it under the tap.

Sylvia was sitting in the dark, her legs drawn up, covered by the blanket.

'I brought you some water.'

Brera tried to discern the outline of her face in the darkness.

'Thanks.'

'Your voice sounds good.'

'Fantastic.'

'I'm being serious.'

'So am I.'

'Sam said you didn't touch your dinner.'

'Sam says put your hands in the air.' She raised both hands and waved them above her head.

'Don't be silly.'

Brera offered her the glass. 'I brought you some water.'

'Thanks.'

Sylvia took the glass. Brera watched her. 'Don't you want it?'

'Give me a minute!'

Brera sighed. 'You want to go back in your bedroom?'

'Obviously.'

'You can soon, but not yet.'

Sylvia scowled.

'Are you upset about Sam and me going away? Because you're welcome to come too, if you feel fit enough.'

'Yeah.'

'What does that mean?'

'I just want to be left alone.'

Brera sensed that she had already outstayed her welcome. 'I'll be in the kitchen, then.'

'Good.'

She turned to leave and Sylvia said, 'I'll have a bath.'

Brera was surprised. 'You had one on Monday.'

'I'll have another one.'

'I'll check the water's hot.'

When she'd gone, Sylvia inspected the glass of water. She sniffed it and then screwed up her face into an expression of intense distaste. She was thirsty. She poked out her tongue and tentatively dipped it into the glass, then quickly withdrew it. 'Soap.'

She pinched her nose between her finger and thumb, gulped down three or four mouthfuls then shook her head and blinked. 'Chemicals.'

Every glass of tap water in London had been through at least twenty other people. For a while she tried to imagine the people that this particular glassful had been through, then turned her mind to more pressing issues.

Now what? Secrets. She had a small batch of them. First, the girl in the park. Second, tasting and smelling. Third, Sam's friend. He said . . . What did he say? He said he wouldn't say anything.

She chuckled. Having secrets made her feel proud and maternal. Her gut felt full of an unspecified mystery. Like she had

143

a pearl inside her, forming, layer by layer. She stopped smiling.

Things must return to normal. They mustn't know. They must go.

She listened as Brera cleaned the bath and set the taps running.

FIFTEEN

What time was it? Four a.m.?

Ruby shifted in her sleep and muttered, 'I don't want this to end.'

In her dream she couldn't open her eyes. Everything was too bright, and when she tried to open her eyes – the effort involved was enormous – the light made her eyes ache, as though she were staring at the sun.

But it didn't matter. She could see perfectly clearly elsewhere, inside her head, in another compartment.

In this compartment it was dark and warm and everything smelled of wet dog. Everything felt like wet dog.

Someone was breathing. She turned to see who it was, but it was too dark.

Where am I?

Maybe . . . She tried to make sense of things. Maybe I'm out swimming. The water is hot. I'm out swimming and now I've climbed from the water on to a rock, inside a cave. The cave is warm and damp. The rock is covered in a soft, woolly seaweed.

She felt it against her skin and it made her skin tingle.

Someone was next to her. She tried to open her eyes, to stare, yet when she opened her eyes the light was too bright, so she closed them again. But this is a different dream. In this dream I can see everything.

Next to her, on the rock, was a dog – a big soggy dog. She turned her head and stared at it. Vincent! She laughed. It wasn't a dog at all. He glared at her. She realized that she was naked.

He said, 'I'm going to have to throw you in.'

His voice was so soft. Obviously the cave has made his voice softer, she thought.

He grabbed her arm. Is he wearing anything? She tried to see,

145

but when she opened her eyes everything was too bright. She felt him touch her breasts and then her belly. Again he said, 'I'm going to have to throw you in.'

'All right.' She giggled. Her voice sounded stupid.

He was pulling her towards the water. She wasn't afraid. She wanted him to pull her in. He was holding her arm, still holding it, but now she was holding his too. She said, 'If I go, you go.'

She sensed the water close to her feet, surrounding her feet, her shins, her calves, her knees. She tried to slide in quicker, but he held her back. She felt his skin all wet and shuddered.

When she awoke her pillow was on the floor. She reached out for it, keeping her eyes closed.

Oh no. I won't wake up from this.

Connor dragged the telephone into his bedroom. He had just made a cup of tea, tip-toeing around the flat so as not to wake anyone. Sarah had a guest. He didn't want to intrude. The telephone cord was just about long enough. He slipped it underneath his door, pushed the door shut, then sat down on the floor and drank a mouthful of his tea. He coughed. It was still too hot. He put the cup down and dialled Sam's number.

It rang several times and then she answered it. He shoved some hair behind his ear. 'So you're up?'

'Yes.'

Already – it had only been three days – it felt strange to her: his voice, his manner so familiar.

He said, 'We haven't spoken in ages.'

'How's Sarah?'

'Pretty busy. Someone stayed over.'

'Who?'

'God knows. A man.'

Sam jerked at the phone cord so hard that she almost disconnected the call.

He was irritated. He thought, What does it matter? It's only *her*.

He said, 'Sarah mentioned that you had some gigs lined up.'

'Hull on Saturday.'

She sounded half-hearted. He noticed and tried to flatter himself that he was the cause of her misery.

Sam said, 'You were in the paper today. A picture and everything.'

'I saw it.' He was pleased that she'd seen it. 'We've got a gig tomorrow too. Subterrania.'

'That's good.'

'Could I see you tonight? You left some stuff here.'

'I don't think so. Sylvia's not been well. We want to spend some time with her before we go.'

'Oh.'

'I'd better get off the phone. I don't want to wake her.'

'I hope it goes well tomorrow,' he said, sounding disconsolate.

'Thanks. See you.' She hung up.

Sylvia coughed. Sam turned. 'Did I wake you?'

'You always have to use me as an excuse. I hate it.'

'Oh. I'm sorry.'

'You both make me sick. You and Brera. You're always doing it.'

'We don't mean to.'

Sam's eyes were fully adjusted to the darkness. She could see Sylvia propped up on the sofa, surrounded by cushions.

'That's the worst part of it, though. You always mean everything you do.'

Sam went back to her room. She sat on her bed and promptly burst into tears. She kept thinking, What's going on? I can't make sense of this. I don't want to make sense of it.

Sylvia padded quietly into the hallway and listened to Sam crying. Good, she thought, that's her out of the way. She could hear Brera brushing her teeth in the bathroom.

She slipped along the passage and into the kitchen. It was so bright in here. She blinked for several seconds before she could adjust her eyes.

The paper was open on the kitchen table. She paged through it, hoping for a familiar face, an image she could recognize, but nothing sprang out at her. She turned to the front and looked for some indication of content. She found what she was searching for and turned towards the back.

Half-way down this page was the heading STIR-FINE! and a picture. She stared at the picture, her eyes widening in surprise. He looked absolutely nothing like he sounded, nothing like she'd imagined.

She was disturbed by a movement in the hallway. She spun away from the paper towards the sink, picked up a glass and held it under the tap.

Brera walked in. 'I thought you were Sam.'

She didn't reply.

'What're you doing?'

'What does it look like?'

'What's wrong?'

'Nothing's bloody wrong!'

She banged the glass down on the draining-board and marched out. She felt dizzy. In the sunlight everything smelled so acute, so strong. Even the newspaper, like bleach and ink – a hot, savage smell.

She was so hungry but she couldn't eat. If I eat, she thought, I might give myself away.

She threw herself on to the sofa. Everything needs to be normal, she decided. She lay down flat. I'm threatened. By what? Alternatives. I must get *back* . . . the feathers, the fluttering, the catch in my throat. No senses, no sense.

She remembered Connor's face: unshaven, so dirty, all that hair, in tangles. She thought, He kept my secret. Now I owe him something. Now we owe each other something. This notion depressed her.

She coughed for a while and then spat out the phlegm from her mouth on to a tissue. Suddenly she found it hard to swallow phlegm, to do normal things.

Maybe God is punishing me for killing that little girl. Everything is getting bigger and bigger, and the bigger everything gets, the smaller I am.

She felt minuscule.

*

Vincent was strolling down Argyll Street with an open can of lager in his hand and a paper under his arm. He was happy. If you ask for anything, he was thinking, you face the possibility of someone saying yes and of someone saying no. This didn't strike him as good enough. It didn't satisfy him.

Pigeons were everywhere: oily, skinny, puffy, mottled. He kicked up his feet as he walked, as if he were striding through winter leaves.

What kind of a commitment had he made to her? Any? None?

Ruby pondered these questions as she worked the till and the pay-out. Friday was Dawn's half-day. As usual, it was busy.

Two-thirty now. Was the dog still all right? She'd nipped out at twelve and had taken her for a short stroll. She'd been going stir-crazy.

Where was he? Sod him.

Where was he, though?

There he was. She felt. Sick.

Two forty-five. He was going to do something she didn't want him to do. The bastard. She'd said no to him, over and over, but he was still here, like he'd threatened. He wore her hat and a pair of almond-shaped mirror glasses. Where did he get hold of those? He looked absurd.

Jason was busy. She checked furtively. He was filling out a stationery order.

'The whole idea,' she'd said, 'is stupid. People rip off book-makers all the time and they always get caught.'

'Only the ones you hear about.'

'But even the ones I hear about have better ideas than yours.'

'How?'

'Well, either way I come out of it looking like I've made a mistake.'

'A small mistake. I bet you make mistakes like that all the time.'

'Not on purpose.'

*

He had chosen his horse: Origami. She'd never even heard of it. Just before the off, when it was busy, he came up and handed her his slip. A queue of punters formed behind him. Jason was giving her a hand, working the other till.

She took the slip from him. This was stupid. She'd told him she wouldn't do it. She'd said so, but now she was doing it. He'd said that he wouldn't write out the slip properly. That was part of the scheme. Only the horse's name and a two, two noughts, in the wrong box. Under pounds instead of pence.

She pushed the slip into her till, pressed a two, kept her finger on the nought button that little bit too long. God! She did it. Registered the bet, tore it in half, handed him his half. He gave her no money.

'What do you call it?' he'd asked. 'The technical name.'

'An over-ring. If your hand slips, or if you don't remember to put in the decimal point at the right time.'

'You wouldn't notice a mistake like that straight away, not if you were busy.'

'I would.'

'I bet you've done it before, though.'

'Accidentally.'

'If the horse wins, you say I gave you the two hundred. Pay your till back with part of the winnings. If I lose, say it was an over-ring.'

The swine, she thought. How many times did I tell him I wouldn't do it?

The race was off. She stood up. How long would it last? Six furlongs?

'Jason,' she said, 'I want to get a Coke.'

She walked past the safety door, through the shop and outside.

'Jason would be bound to recognize you if you came up to collect the money.'

'I'd get someone else to collect it.'

'Who? I wouldn't want anyone else involved.'

'Nobody.'

'Anyway, if I take a bet worth over fifty quid I'm supposed to notify the manager.'

'Not if you're too busy.'

'Even then.'

She picked up two crates, placed one on top of the other and sat down. It was warm here. The sun shone on her bare arms and her face.

'What's the point?'

'You could buy the dog. They treat you like shit anyway.'

'Even the thought of it makes me feel sick.'

'That's excitement.'

The crates were uncomfortable. They cut into her legs. Vincent tapped her on the shoulder. For an instant she thought he was a wasp, a hornet. She jerked away.

'I told you I didn't want to do this. I said no.'

And he'd punished her by staying away. She had been punished.

I'm not nice after all, she realized, only weak. Weak. That was an ugly word. It made her feel ugly.

'The horse won,' he said, grinning. 'At five-to-one. Origami. I chose it because my sister used to make origami swans.'

She looked up at him. 'I said I didn't want to do this.'

She couldn't see his eyes, only her own face reflected in his glasses. A weak mouth. A weak chin. A weak face.

'But you did it.'

'I'm fidelity-bonded. Do you know what that means?'

'No.'

'It means that if I ever get caught doing anything illegal, I can never work with money again. Not anywhere, ever again.'

He scowled at her. Maybe she just wasn't clever enough.

'I've earned you eight hundred pounds. The horse came in at five-to-one.'

'I don't want your money.'

'Not my money, your money.'

'I don't want the money. You have it.'

'I don't need it.'

'Then burn it.'

She stood up and walked back inside.

When she sat down again, Jason said, 'There's a bet here for two hundred. You should've told me you'd taken it before the off.'

'It was on the off. I didn't have time.'

He handed her the slip, settled, with the amount she had to pay out written in red ink at the bottom. She stacked ten bundles of hundreds into a neat pile and waited for Vincent to come back in. He didn't come.

She settled other bets, took slips, counted money, handed it over. She waited. She took a slip, counted the money, took a slip . . .

Vincent's writing. She looked up. A face she almost recognized. Not Vincent's face. She picked up the bundles she'd prepared and handed them over, two hundred short. He took the money and thanked her. The spare two hundred she moved into her till.

She knew that face. Who was he?

Fuck.

Sam noticed something strange about Sarah's complexion as soon as she met her. A roughness. A reddish, blotchy patch around her mouth, nose and on her chin.

They were at the Scala watching a matinée showing of the director's cut of *Pretty Baby*. Sarah's idea. Sam had been keen to talk, which was unfortunate.

'How's Connor?'

'Himself. Loud.'

'Have you been busy?'

'No.'

'Do you like Brooke Shields?'

'Sometimes.'

That redness. She had been kissing someone. With stubble. That would explain it.

She took the dog out, made something to eat, began packing. Only a small bag for the time being.

Vincent arrived while she was feeding the dog. He thumped on the door and then pushed it open.

'You should be careful. I walked straight in here from the street.'

She wanted to silence him for a minute so that she could yell at him, but he kept on talking.

'This small guy was sweeping the stairs. He stopped me and was asking all kinds of questions. Wanted to know about the dog.'

'The caretaker. Red hair.'

'That's him.'

He walked into the bathroom. She heard him turning on the taps. She returned to her bedroom and sat down on her bed. She listened to the sound the water made as it hit the enamel bath. She listened to laughter, conversation, arguments going on outside in the street. She listened to the noises the dog made, pushing her bowl around on the kitchen tiles with her nose.

A while later Vincent appeared in the doorway, wrapped only in a towel.

'What are you doing?'

'Packing.'

She was packed.

'You aren't really going to Hackney?'

'I said I would.'

'You should've kept that money.'

'You told me,' she said, very calmly, 'that you didn't even know that epileptic.'

'Who?'

'Don't fuck me around.'

'I actually just met him again today.'

'You set me up.'

Vincent's expression, previously churlish, became serious. 'You don't honestly think that?'

She knew it. She knew it.

What could he do with her? She had shocked him.

They were both silent for a while. She was staring down at her hands.

Eventually she looked up at him. He had dropped his towel. Her eyes widened.

'Is it just sex you want?' he said, his voice sounding flat and angry. 'Is that it?'

She wasn't surprised by this question. The only thing that surprised her was his honesty. But he was always honest. That was the problem.

'Look at me,' he said, 'I'm ridiculous.'

She did look at him. She straightened her back and crossed her arms. He didn't appear to be upset or embarrassed by her scrutiny. His skin was pink-tinged from the heat of the bath. His body was surprisingly hairy. He looked overweight. His stomach protruded. His thighs were stocky and angular. He said, 'Don't you want to laugh? Don't I make you want to laugh?'

As he spoke she was staring at his penis, which seemed unusually pale, a whitish-blue colour by comparison with the ruddy tone of the rest of his skin. His testicles were lopsided.

She stood up and unbuttoned the shirt she was wearing. 'You made me do something I didn't want to do.'

'What?'

She took off her shirt, hooked her thumbs into the black leggings she wore, pulled them down, stepped out of them, unclipped her bra, pulled down her knickers.

He noticed that her skin was a very cheap white and that her hips were fleshy and strong. Her nipples were tiny and a pale beige colour, like small round servings of coffee ice-cream.

Now what? There was something in her expression, something harsh and hostile.

He said, 'Why are you doing this?'

'I'm sick of you taking advantage. What did you do with that money?'

She was crazy for him, but he'd made her hate herself. Somehow.

154

He had never seen a woman strip as an act of hostility before. He wondered whether that was how she saw his body – as something offensive – when all he'd really intended was to ridicule himself.

'I let him have it. It felt like he was owed it. I don't know.'

In the same way, in the same way that he'd not wanted her to touch him, to kiss him, in that casual manner she had, that easy, accidental fashion. He didn't want to be like the dog. A mistake. He either wanted plain sex, or, plain sex, or . . . He never thought about these things. Never. He couldn't think about them.

He picked up his towel and walked out. She climbed into bed.

SIXTEEN

When Brera found Sylvia early on Saturday morning, she was huddled in an ungainly heap by her bedroom door, clutching a partially unbent coat-hanger and a fish-knife.

Brera prodded her with a slippered toe and said grimly, 'Now what? Is this how it's going to be?'

Sylvia stirred and then turned over. She opened her eyes. 'I want to go in again. We agreed, didn't we? You locked me out before and it didn't work.'

'Twice.'

Brera clearly remembered these two occasions. On the first – Sylvia had been thirteen – she'd gone on hunger strike: eight days without food before Brera relented. On the second occasion – at fifteen – after three days outside she'd sliced her arms with a kitchen knife. Brera didn't really want to dwell on either incident. This time, she'd decided, it wouldn't come to that. She said tersely, 'Are you warning me? Is that it?'

'I'm not doing anything. I can do exactly as I please.'

'Listen to your voice. It sounds so clear.'

'I don't care.'

'Have you eaten?' Brera was keen to avoid a confrontation.

'No.'

'Why aren't you eating?'

Sylvia sat up, leaned her back against the door and rapidly changed tack. 'I did eat, earlier on, before I fell asleep.'

'What did you eat?'

'Some bread. An apple. Milk.'

'That's not enough. I'll get you some cereal.'

'I'm full.'

Sylvia patted her stomach and looked off sideways. Brera found her expression shifty and devious. She's still such a child, she thought, as she squatted down next to her and put out a hand to touch her hair. 'You know we won't go if you don't want us to. That woman, Ruby, is coming this morning at eight. Maybe you don't like her?'

'She's all right.'

'You don't really want us to go.'

Sylvia's hair felt like wire under her hand. Sylvia turned and squinted up into her face. 'You want to blame me for not wanting to go yourself. I can see straight through you. But I won't have you blaming me again. I just want . . . I only want to be left alone, that's all.'

Brera drew back her hand and stood up. 'You're going to do something stupid. I can tell.'

'I won't do anything. I just want . . .'

'I know what you want. Just give it two more days. I want you to recover properly.'

'Give me the key.' Sylvia put out her hand.

'I'll give the key to Ruby. I'll instruct her to let you in on Tuesday. That's a promise.'

'It's too long.'

'Only two days.'

Brera tried not to sound brutal. She knew that with Sylvia a fine line had to be drawn between cooperation and coercion.

Very gently Sylvia said, 'I'm lonely. Please let me in.'

'No.' Brera's voice remained sure and calm. 'Tuesday's soon enough.'

Sylvia crossed her arms. 'You always have to treat me like a child.'

'You always have to behave like one.'

'OK.' She stood up, scowling, her face reddening. 'We'll see.'

She turned and stalked away, down the corridor and into the living-room. Seconds later, Brera could hear her opening the curtains.

She called out after her, 'Are you trying to spoil things? Are you punishing me?'

After a short silence Sylvia shouted back, 'Only God can punish you.'

157

Brera scratched her head and then inspected her finger-nails. Eventually she said, 'You don't even believe in God, you bloody hypocrite.'

Sylvia grinned to herself, then sat down on the sofa. Why am I grinning? she wondered. I've got nothing to grin about.

There was a mustiness in the room that made her want to sneeze. She listened out to hear what Brera would do next. She crossed her fingers, hoping that she wouldn't try to bring her something to eat, then uncrossed them with a small sigh of relief as she heard her go into Sam's bedroom.

It felt strange having the curtains open. Over the past four or so days she'd spent all her time in virtual darkness. Early on she'd had trouble working out why this was so, but had felt too ill to do anything about it. Now she stared at the window, looking for her birds. Maybe they've forgotten me? If they have, I might just as well be dead.

She blinked several times, growing gradually more accustomed to the light.

When had the sun risen? Two hours, three hours earlier?

She sniffed and then sneezed. In the bright light she could see dust floating in the air: thousands of specks of it. She tried not to breathe them in, then felt light-headed, so filled her lungs. She could smell the sunlight. It smelled like a big, black oil slick – warm and oozy.

When she'd been talking to Brera, she'd been struck by how pungent her perfume was. Like dried apricots – a sweet, harsh smell. She thought, It smelled so strong as her hand touched my hair, I thought I'd gag.

The sunlight began to upset her. She debated whether to close the curtains again, but became too fearful, too frightened in case the birds had forgotten her. Several had accumulated on the window-sill – three sparrows and a starling. She couldn't be sure, though, that they wouldn't have been there anyway. She peered at them, over the arm of the sofa, too overwhelmed by the new, hot, hazy, dazy smells in the room to walk over.

Her mind switched to the night's activities: the coat-hanger and the fish-knife. *The smell from her room!* She'd noticed it before, of course, but she hadn't realized quite how *repulsive* . . . She couldn't think about it. Too dangerous.

She lay down and closed her eyes. It was that time of day: cars full of people, driving to work, trains, tubes and buses. She could smell the exhaust fumes, like a thick, yellowy grog – a horrible, tepid, burning smell. The smell of business, of a big cigar.

If only I could hibernate. Draw in my head like a tortoise. Get into a dark cave, like a bear and simply sleep.

Two days, she thought. They won't get me this way.

Sam had overheard the conversation in the hallway. She was lying in bed. She'd been awake for several hours; had, in fact, been listening to Sylvia earlier, working away at the lock on her bedroom door.

As she lay there she wondered whether Brera was intending to talk her way out of going on the tour. At the last minute.

She tried to think about Connor, but couldn't concentrate on him, his feelings, the possibility of having hurt him.

She tried to think about Sarah, but, again, couldn't settle her thoughts.

If I loved her. Loved, she thought, still smarting, my face, my figure, all that would be wasted. And then, What a stupid way to think.

Brera tapped on Sam's door and walked in. Sam opened her eyes. 'What's wrong?'

Brera closed the door, walked over and sat down on the end of her bed.

Sam propped herself up on her elbows. Brera's hair was tied back into a scruffy pony-tail. She untied it and then massaged her scalp with the tips of her fingers. As she did this she said, 'You've been distracted lately.'

Sam was surprised that they were suddenly discussing her and not Sylvia.

'So?'

Had Brera noticed anything? Her heart felt like a sparrow – small, light, fluttering.

'You're uptight because you think I'm going to back out of the tour at the last minute.'

Sam relaxed, was relieved at her mother's lack of insightfulness. She said calmly, 'Things have a way of sorting themselves out.'

Brera stopped fiddling with her hair and started to speak again, but Sam's mind was elsewhere: I'm missing something. It's true. I'm missing something but I don't know what. Something's wrong. I'm incomplete.

She was miserable.

Brera was saying, 'There comes a time when you have to let a person take responsibility for their own life. Otherwise it's like a kind of cruelty.'

Sam listened to this string of words as though they were being spoken on the surface of a pool, above water, and she was floating, just underneath, submerged, her ears full of liquid.

Am I different? I want to be the same, but now I feel . . . separate.

This was Sarah's fault. Were men the same as women after all? Was she being like a man? Was that how she felt?

Brera was saying, 'I won't have her dying in my house. She can go and die somewhere else. She's old enough to. She's got to start being courteous.'

Sam rubbed her face. Small dots of sleep were encrusted in the corners of each eye, like tiny scraps of wheat. She picked them out and then said, 'So go and tell her.'

She felt amoral. Removed. She didn't care what happened.

Brera stood up. 'I'll get packed first.'

'Go now.'

'You're right.'

When Brera had gone, Sam lay down in bed again. She thought, I am different.

And what could be worse than that?

Sarah wasn't yet dressed. Her long legs stuck out from her dressing-gown. To Connor they looked thin and ungainly, like the limbs of a deer, but white.

'Sam's like a tiny goddess,' she said, provoking him. 'I don't believe she ever invests in anything emotionally. She's invulnerable, which means that she wants to understand things but not to feel them. She's incapable of genuine involvement.'

Connor was trying to eat his cereal. He ignored Sarah. She loved it when he ignored her. It meant that she could say anything, that she had beaten him, defeated him, had won, was winning or would win.

He picked up a cup of scalding hot coffee, holding the cup itself, not the handle. It was burning him. He continued to ignore her. She was only a parrot, chattering. How strange it is, he thought, when things that are extremes come together. He used all his energy to convince himself that what his fingers felt was a freezing sensation instead of a burning one.

Sam was perched on the edge of her bed playing the guitar. The noise she made drowned out the sound of raised voices from elsewhere in the flat. Above the guitar she could only hear a vague squawking sound, a frantic bickering, like the call of a starling.

She wore a loose pair of brown dungarees, the straps of which nestled in the crook of each arm. The front bib had tipped down too, revealing her left breast in its entirety. She knew how beautiful she must look, like this. But it gave her no joy and no comfort.

She continued to play, remembering as she strummed something that Sylvia had said about birdsong. She'd said, 'If you listen to a thrush sing, you can hear how birds use a musical scale which contains far more intervals within the octave than our scale. Our system is a kind of compromise. We cancel out all those extra tones so that we're left with a practical scale of twelve. Birds have a completely different musical language. We can listen to it, but we can't understand it. And it's only because of the way that we've chosen to transcribe music. We made it incomprehensible, on purpose. We decided.'

The doorbell rang. She stopped strumming and listened to the sudden silence in the flat. She put down her guitar.

*

161

Brera welcomed Ruby inside and pointed her towards an armchair in the living-room. To Ruby the flat seemed different: lighter. Doors and curtains were open. She dumped her suitcase and sat down, holding on firmly to the dog by her collar. She sensed an atmosphere. Brera wore no make-up but her cheeks were red. Sylvia seemed, if anything, even smaller than during their last encounter – anaemic, a pale yellow, her every feature like so many tucks and pleats in a piece of pastry.

Sylvia spoke: 'That dog stinks of dog.'

Sam appeared in the doorway. 'That's a tautology. Well, nearly.'

Sylvia's eyes flickered over towards her and then away.

Sam smiled at Ruby. 'Hi.'

Ruby smiled back and said, 'Are you all packed yet? Has Steven called?'

'No, but I should think he'll be here soon.'

Brera was staring out of the window, watching a small congregation of sparrows who had assembled under the eaves of the roof outside.

Sam said gently, 'We'd better get a move on.'

Brera snapped to attention. 'I'll get changed. Then I'll pack.' She turned to Ruby. 'I've scribbled down a few instructions. I left them in the kitchen on the table.'

Ruby nodded, hoping that things would be organized before nine-thirty. She couldn't afford to be late for work again.

Sam and Brera disappeared. Sylvia sat cross-legged on the sofa. As soon as Brera was out of earshot she said, 'I won't be any trouble.'

'I'm sure we'll be fine.'

Ruby felt uneasy.

'Maybe you should give the dog some water?'

Ruby stood up. 'Good idea.' She pulled the dog along the corridor, past Sylvia's room – the smell was as bad, if not worse, than on her last visit – and into the kitchen. Sam was here, making tea. She put three cups on a tray and passed a fourth one over to Ruby. Ruby took it and sat down.

When Sam had gone, she tried to convince herself that her life

162

was a broad expanse, a large space, like a field, which Vincent only fitted into in a very small way – on the horizon, a figure on a distant hill, a scarecrow, a small, insubstantial dot.

Sam took Sylvia a cup of tea. Sylvia motioned her to put it down a distance away, on the floor.

Sam did as she was instructed and then said, 'How many days has it been since your last asthma attack? Four? Listen to your breathing. The difference is amazing.'

Sylvia's nostrils twitched as she smelled the steam rising from the cup of tea, which stank of curdled milk, sour milk mixed up with a sharp scent of tannin. It disgusted her.

She stared up at Sam. 'The thing is,' she said, calculatedly mournful, 'I'm not happy.'

Sam couldn't help chuckling. 'Are you serious? You? Not happy? You're never happy.'

Sylvia's eyes began to water, entirely of their own accord. Everything overwhelmed her. Usually things overwhelmed her and she was passive. She *chose* to be. But this was different. She felt helpless and impotent. When she tried to speak, her voice emerged as a tiny, timorous squeak. 'No matter what I say or do, it makes no difference. No wonder I feel angry. No wonder I want to hurt myself.'

'Shut-up!' Sam moved towards her and placed a hand across her mouth, gagging her, feeling the damp warmth of her lips and saliva against her palm.

Sam's voice had sounded ferocious, but she didn't feel at all angry. Instead she felt frightened; mainly for Brera, but for herself too. Sylvia's eyes widened but she didn't move. Sam kept her hand where it was and said quietly, 'Don't ruin everything just because you know you can. Consider us. Imagine how we feel.'

She removed her hand, inspecting it for a second – as though the hand was somehow separate from her body, from herself – and then wiped it on the front of her dungarees before turning and leaving the room.

Once Sam had gone, Sylvia took hold of the bottom of her T-shirt, pulled it up and rubbed her face vigorously with it. When

163

she'd finished rubbing, her face was crumpled and wrinkled, as though she wanted to howl, or was howling, but without making a sound. She looked like a tiny red ant.

After a while her expression returned to normal. She whispered, 'What did she have on her hands? What sort of perfume? Like vanilla pods. Like terrible vanilla on a knife blade.'

She was calm now, outside, but inside she was wild, galled and hot with anger.

I've got to hurt them back. But hurt them without hurting myself. That's how people behave. That's what Brera wants.

She stared over towards the window, but for once the birds – on the sill, in the sky, perched on the power lines – didn't seem like everything, didn't fill her world. Suddenly she felt the need to make room for something else. To broaden her horizons.

He'd already been awoken once by the phone.

At half-past eight the doorbell rang. He staggered up from the sofa to answer it, feeling like his spine had been twisted during the course of the night into a voluptuous spiral. He held the base of his back with one hand, endeavouring to massage the offending area, while with his other hand he clutched walls, doors and banisters, trying to support himself. Eventually he reached the front door. He opened it.

Steven stood there, smartly attired in a light-green suit. His lapels were wide, and his tie too. The tie was decorated with tropical fruit: a mango, kumquats, grapes and a papaya.

Vincent gingerly put out his hand and took hold of the tie. 'You weren't obliged to wear that.'

Steven knocked his hand away. 'Has Ruby gone yet?'

Vincent tried to remember whether he'd seen Ruby or not. He shook his head. 'I've been asleep. Someone phoned her early on.'

He attempted to call to mind his earlier phone conversation. Steven, meanwhile, pushed past him and bounded upstairs. Vincent closed the door and followed him at a more genteel pace.

He walked into the flat and closed the door behind him. Steven emerged from the bedroom. 'Some of her things are gone.'

Vincent scratched his head. 'Someone phoned this morning. What's the time?'

Steven checked his watch. 'Eight-thirty.'

'Don.'

'Who?'

'The man who phoned. Don. He said it was important. Will you be seeing her?'

'I hope so.'

'Good.' Vincent sat down on the sofa. 'You can tell her, then.'

Steven appraised Vincent from above. He inspected the cut on his hairline. After a few moments he said, 'I suppose this means you won't be seeing her again.'

'Ruby?' Vincent thought for a second. 'Probably.'

Steven couldn't tell whether this 'probably' meant yes or no. To try to ascertain which, he said, 'How long were you planning to stay here?'

Vincent rubbed his forehead. His fingers followed the path of his scar, his scab. Steven winced as he watched this, worrying that he might try to pull the scab off. He did try, but the cut was still too new.

Steven didn't like the idea that Vincent might be planning to stay on in the flat indefinitely. 'Doesn't it bother you that she's gone?'

Vincent yawned. 'She's left most of her stuff. She's left her records.'

'That was kind of her.'

Vincent realized that he wasn't particularly enjoying this conversation. He didn't want to analyse his feelings, preferring instead to feel urges and to act upon them.

'You *like* Ruby?' Steven asked, trying not to sound too sarcastic.

'What?' Vincent almost laughed. 'What kind of a question is that?'

At the same time, however, he thought, Caring and liking. Are they the same things? Can I like a person without really caring about them? He supposed so.

Steven walked back over to the bedroom and peered in

165

through the door. The whole flat looked like a tip. He turned towards Vincent. 'Before you go, can you tidy the place up? It's a mess.'

Vincent shrugged. 'She likes it like this. She made this mess.'

He pulled his legs up on to the sofa and lay down on it again, closing his eyes. He didn't want to talk about Ruby any more. He found discussing her with Steven depressing. He didn't like the idea, which any type of conversation between them implied, of some kind of common ground, something shared, any sort of similarity between them.

There's nothing to discuss. I won't commit myself to any one thing, to one place, one idea, one person. I have to commit myself to everything. If it'd only been sex – at first I thought it'd only be sex – then it would've been fine. Now everything's too confused. People shouldn't need to demand things from each other.

He liked this idea. He said, 'People shouldn't expect too much from each other.'

Steven was staring over towards the door, thinking about leaving, but at the same time peculiarly dissatisfied by this interlude with Vincent. When Vincent spoke, Steven couldn't understand what he meant. He paused and waited for Vincent to clarify his words. Vincent kept his eyes closed. He was smiling to himself.

'What a wanker,' Steven muttered, letting himself out and going down the stairs.

After Steven had gone, Vincent continued to smile. He was remembering the colour of Ruby's nipples.

The day stretched ahead of him. He knew that he was at liberty to fill it in any way he chose.

Ruby put her head down on the table, using her folded arms as a cushion. She closed her eyes.

'You're not ill or anything, are you?'

'No.' She didn't bother opening her eyes or lifting her head. It's only Steven, she thought, and he doesn't count.

Steven pulled out a chair and sat down. Ruby listened to the dog as she shifted nervously under the table, concerned at his proximity.

'I just went to your flat.'

'Why?'

'I was going to give you a lift. Your friend was still there.'

'Vincent.'

'He said that Don phoned and that I should tell you. Does that make any sense?'

Ruby opened her eyes. 'Don? Why?'

'Didn't say.' He registered her expression. 'You can ring back now if it's important.'

'No. I'll ring him later.'

She calculated in her mind the number of days that had expired since she'd acquired the dog. Six. Her mind turned to Vincent and the money. When she'd said no, had she really meant no? Maybe then, but now?

Steven said quietly, 'You'll be all right here, won't you?'

'Yeah. I should think so.'

He looked at his watch. 'Are you working? It's nearly half-nine.'

'I'd like to go soon, but it won't look too good if I leave before they do.'

He pushed back his chair and stood up. 'I'll try and hurry them up a bit. They shouldn't be much longer.'

She popped her head under the table and addressed the dog: 'I'm going out soon. Can you hold your bladder for eight hours? I hope so.'

She hoped so.

Several pieces of paper were on the telephone table, some in a neat pile, others crammed into the directory. Eventually Sylvia found what she was looking for: a small piece of lemon-yellow notepaper. On it, in Sam's hand, Connor's name in capital letters and the ten digits of his phone number. She dialled.

It rang three times and was then answered: 'Hi. This is Connor.'

'Sylvia.' Her voice was clear and loud.

'You sound completely different from the last time we spoke.'

'So?'

'I was just saying. Why did you ring?'

Sylvia felt silly. She hated taking the initiative.

'I want you to come and pick me up.'

'What?'

She repeated what she had said, shaping the consonants and vowels slowly and carefully as though speaking to a child: 'I said, I want you to come around here and pick me up.'

'Why?'

'I want to visit your flat. Sam told me all about it. She told me how nice it was.'

'She did?' Connor was incredulous.

Sylvia grimaced to herself. She thought men must be very stupid.

'Will you come?'

He hesitated and then acquiesced: 'Maybe I could just visit you. How would that be?'

She scowled. 'Come now,' and cut him off.

She stood up. Her head felt too light. The walls slipped slightly and the carpet wavered. She closed her eyes for a moment and tried to focus herself.

Forty minutes later Sylvia stood damp and naked in Brera's room, staring into the dressing-table mirror. She'd had a bath and had washed her hair, which was wrapped up in a towelling turban.

Her naked body looked awful. Her hip and rib bones jutted out under her yellowy skin, the bones far too clear, too evident. Her breasts were small but droopy, like tiny bread rolls in two translucent plastic bags.

She inspected the stretch marks on her breasts, belly and buttocks, the small clusters of eczema on her arms and chest, on her hands and neck and on the arches of her feet. She wasn't particularly self-conscious, didn't care what people thought. She rarely tried to see herself as others saw her. She continued to stare at herself, her expression blank and uncritical. The air was warm.

She left the room for a while, then reappeared, minutes later, fully dressed. She wore one of Sam's dresses: a slightly old-fashioned, loose-fitting brown pinafore dress, which reached to well below her calves. Underneath it she wore a pea-green T-shirt. Her legs were bare, and on her feet were her old brown sandals.

She threw her head forward – an action which occasioned a wave of dizzy nausea – pulled off the towel, using it to rub dry the ends of her hair, then opened the top drawer of Brera's dressing-table. The sweet aroma of perfume and make-up which rose from the drawer forced her to step back for a moment. These smells shot straight up her nose and made it run. She sniffed and stepped determinedly closer again, holding her nose between finger and thumb this time and breathing through her mouth. She looked for make-up and creams which were unperfumed, and applied these products to her face with caution.

When she'd finished, she stepped back, pushed her hands through her hair, pulling down her wiry curls into some semblance of order, and inspected herself in the mirror. Her face still looked gaunt, thin, strangely moonish. She smiled. Her teeth were yellow. Over the past few days she'd been unable to put toothpaste – that sweet, awful, pungent stuff – into her mouth.

She closed the drawer, dusted down her pinafore and then walked into the hallway, pausing for a moment to listen to the scuffling, snorting sounds that the dog was making in the kitchen. She walked to her bedroom door, waited, held her breath, but could hear nothing. No sounds at all.

'I bet that bitch closed my window.'

The *smell*, though! It was still there. It made her head feel like her brain was stewing in vinegar. Of course she was able to smell it everywhere in the house, but here it was concentrated, heady and undiluted.

She returned to the living-room. She was nervous. She walked over to the television, switched it on and turned the volume down. Instead of sitting on the sofa, she primly tucked in her dress and sat down in a small armchair.

As she watched the screen she hummed to herself: snatches of a tune she'd been composing over the past few days. She listened to her own voice, pushed it out and pulled it in. She listened in amazement as the cords in her throat held a note, didn't waver, simply held on to it and expelled it with an alarming purity.

What did this mean? What had changed? She curtailed her thoughts, refusing to contemplate options, choices, possibilities. She didn't need choice. She stopped humming. She listened.

Someone was climbing the stairs outside. Connor. She recognized the sounds he made. He knocked at the door. She stood up and steadied herself by holding on to the arm of the chair.

How many days now since I ate? she wondered, and then, Will I answer or will I just let him knock and knock?

When she felt steady enough, she walked to the door and opened it.

An ambulance was parked on Wardour Street, blocking the one-way system. Its two attendants were uptight. They had struggled along the market with a stretcher, negotiating the stalls, the fruit, the rubbish. Ruby followed them into the shop.

Jason was pointing towards the men's toilets: 'There's a needle about a foot long blocking the cistern in there and blood sprayed all over the wall.'

To Ruby he said, 'Toro found him.'

'Who? Is he dead?'

'Looks like he swallowed his tongue. Toro's in the staff kitchen out back. I said he could make himself some coffee.'

Dawn was holding the toilet door open. Ruby walked over. She had to look. She glanced in. The white urinals. The blue tiles. Her gut turned. He was right. Blood. A bad smell. They were lifting the body. It wasn't even stiff yet. His head rolled back, his face, set, grey, his neck like a slack rope.

'Christ!'

She was sick on to her hand. Out it came, *swish*, on to her hand. Nothing substantial. Only water, saliva.

What had she done? And Vincent. What had he done? She was sick again. Bile and water. Someone would be punished. But who would it be? And how?

When the police came, later on, Dawn spoke to them. She said, 'Yeah, I'd seen him before. Last Saturday, a week ago, I chucked him out of here. He always had a bad habit.'

Connor was dumbfounded when Sylvia opened the door and he saw her for the first time. Like Sam, she was tiny. Bird-like, he thought, smiling. But she was white, not black like Sam, not beautiful. Nevertheless, he enjoyed her expressions. Her face, he decided, was like a security camera, projecting everything internal externally, for immediate perusal.

When she opened the door she peered at him suspiciously. He said, 'I'm Connor.'

'I know.'

Instead of welcoming him inside, she stepped out into the corridor and closed the door behind her. He was irritated by this. 'Couldn't we go in for a while?'

'Sure.' She smiled at him. Her teeth were small and yellow.

He waited for a few seconds but she didn't budge. 'Do you have a key?'

'No.'

She stared at him, as though expecting him to have one, then turned and started off down the stairs.

He followed her. He asked, 'Is someone staying with you? Someone who *does* have a key?'

Sylvia stopped for a moment. 'I've got to go slowly. I can't breathe and talk at the same time. Outside I have to breathe through my mouth.'

As she started to walk again he said, 'Will the birds be a problem out in the open?'

She stopped again. 'Not if someone else is with me. Smaller birds are naturally cautious. Pigeons . . .' She frowned. 'Well, just don't take me to Trafalgar Square.'

They caught a bus. Sylvia breathed through her mouth for the duration. If she could have pinched her nose for the whole trip she would have. The smells – the stink of exhaust fumes, dirt, grime, other people – were appalling.

Physically, Connor found her charming. She was chapped and scuffed, scruffy and mauled, but there was something pure and tiny and strong about her. Obviously he found her terrifying. Obviously, he thought, she's completely mad.

On the tube, something odd happened. As they waited for a train, she put out her hand – a minute hand, dry to the touch, rough, scabby – and took hold of his. His body stiffened. He thought, Why is she doing this? He tried to catch her expression out of the corner of his eye, not turning his head, keen not to confront or embarrass her. He saw that she had her eyes closed. She swayed slightly.

'Are you all right?'

She nodded, still breathing through her mouth.

When the tube arrived, she moved very slowly and heavily. He prayed, God, I know it's selfish, but don't let her die on me. That'd finish me off completely.

At last they were home. By the time they'd arrived, she was panting. He opened the door and followed her in. She walked straight into the living-room and stood in the centre of the carpet, staring around her.

He said, 'I'll get you a drink. I bet your throat's dry after all that . . . breathing.'

'I only want water. Do you have bottled? Not Evian, it's too chalky.'

'My flatmate drinks bottled stuff.'

He went into the kitchen and opened the fridge.

Sylvia remained where she was. She didn't move, just closed her mouth and sniffed tentatively. This room, she decided, stinks of hippie oil. She didn't like it.

Connor returned with a glass of water. He offered her the glass and she took it. He said, 'Why are you pulling that face?'

'This room.' She was breathing through her mouth again. 'It smells like perfume. I don't like it.'

She looked around. 'Where's your room?'

He pointed. The door was half-open. She took several steps in that direction and then her legs began to wobble. He noticed and moved to assist her, taking the glass from her and putting an arm about her waist.

Slowly he helped her into his bedroom and on to his bed. Once comfortably seated, she put her hand out for the glass, took it from him and drained it in several gulps. Some of the water splashed down her chin and on to her pinafore.

He squatted next to her. 'You don't seem very well.'

His head was only a foot or so away from hers. His face, however, was partially covered by hair. His hair looked soft. She liked the way that she could see only a fraction of his features, but also it maddened her. She put out her hand and roughly drew his hair to one side, tucking it behind his ear. His face expressed a mixture of surprise and concern.

She said, 'Let me be honest with you.'

She continued to stare at him and thought, What shall I say? Shall I tell him the truth? Shall I ask him to just leave me alone?

Her face projected her thoughts. He could see that she felt trapped, and was about to offer to leave her for a while, to say this to her, when her stomach interrupted them both with a loud, snarling, watery gurgle.

'How long since you ate?'

She glared at him, as though affronted. 'I won't eat anything.'

He rocked back on to his haunches, surveying her. Am I doing this for Sam? he wondered.

He tried to understand Sylvia, what it was that she thought she was doing. Eventually he said, 'Why have you been breathing through your mouth all this time? Are you still upset by the smell of things? Like you were the other day, on the phone, remember?'

She avoided his gaze, focused on his drums and said, 'Do you play those?'

'How long since you ate anything?'

'Recently.' She answered too quickly.

He said, 'I guess that's why you seem so weak. You've not been eating. Punishing Sam and Brera for going away.'

She laughed. 'I don't care what they do. I have my own life.'

173

He stood up. 'I'm going to make you something to eat, and if you don't eat it, I'm going to throw you out.'

He'd decided that firmness was best. She seemed far too manipulative to tolerate subtlety.

She stared at him coolly. 'I don't mind. I'll go.' She tried to push herself up, but couldn't stand.

'How long since you ate?'

She turned her mind back. 'Thursday morning . . .' then thought some more. Thursday morning she hadn't eaten either. She found it hard to remember her last meal: maybe a sandwich on Wednesday night.

Connor stood up. 'I'll get you something.'

She wanted to stop him. 'Wait a second.'

He paused on the threshold of the room. 'Now what?'

She said, 'I'm the sort of person who likes . . . discomfort. If I feel ill, I feel stronger. Do you understand what I mean?'

She knew this was a ludicrous question, so before he answered she said, 'I could go home.'

'Well, don't expect me to help you. You don't even have any money. How far do you think you'll get in your condition? Be sensible.'

She considered this. She thought, What if I collapse outside and someone calls the police? Maybe they'll have my picture, my description, on their files. Maybe they'll know all about the girl in the park and the geese. Or else . . . Now her mind was speeding. Or else I might collapse and get taken to hospital. They'll call Brera and she'll come back. They'd never forgive me. She and Sam. It'll justify everything they've both said.

She looked up at Connor. 'All right. Get me something.'

She flopped back on to the bed. Connor remained in the doorway long enough to notice that she didn't put her knees together when she lay down, but luckily the fabric of her dress fell between her legs.

She is like a man, he thought, remembering Sarah's comment.

Sylvia stared up at the ceiling. This bed, she decided, smells strange. She could smell Sam on the sheets – a scent of vanilla –

174

but it was mixed with something else. Sex, she decided. His smell.

She found him physically interesting. He was slight and thin, but also tall and in no way gawky. He had sensitive hands. His skin was healthy and smooth. His face wasn't actually handsome, but it was the sort of face a small mammal might have – not a rodent's face – a natural face. Clear and uncomplicated.

Her reverie was spoiled by the smell of real coffee. She felt physical alarm. She sensed her pulse rate quickening. She sniffed the air, inhaled it, digested it. Moments later she differentiated the aroma of bacon – a sweet, spicy smell – and the bland but startling fragrance of an egg frying.

She was cold. She touched her arms, which, she discovered, were rough with goose-pimples. She rubbed these vigorously until they melted away and then pushed herself up into a sitting position. Every sense, every pore, every orifice felt aroused.

Connor piled the coffee, juice and fried breakfast on to a tray and picked it up. He hoped that this combination of food wouldn't be too fatty and rich for someone who hadn't eaten in a while. Porridge would probably have been better for her, he thought, and weak tea. He carried the tray into his bedroom.

Sylvia was no longer on the bed. She was standing behind his drum-kit, staring out of the window.

He put the tray down. 'Come on. Eat it while it's still hot.'

She turned and faced him. Her eyes were wild and round. 'Don't make me.'

He didn't want her mood to infect him. He couldn't help thinking what an affecting person she was. He picked up a knife and sliced into some bacon, into the egg, and scooped these and a couple of slices of mushroom on to a fork. He stepped around his drum-kit and carried this small offering over to her. She pushed herself up against the window, her mouth tightly shut.

'Open up.'

She shook her head, but he noticed her nostrils twitching. The food was inches from her face. Her eyes began to turn back in her skull, rolling, white, like the eyes of a frightened pony. For a second she looked as though she might topple into the window.

175

He put out an arm to support her, curling it around her back. Her mouth opened, and a small moan, a tiny groan, escaped from her lips. He took this opportunity to slip the forkful of food into her mouth, afterwards closing her lips with his fingers.

She tried to swallow and to spit at the same time, staggering sideways, away from him. She put her hands over her ears, as though taste were sound and sound was too, too full of flavour. Something exploded within her, like an engine firing in her mouth, starting up, revving itself, gathering energy, a sensation so violent, so total, so acute, that she could only close her eyes and shake her head and think about screaming, but not scream because her mouth was too full, her head was too full. Again she tried to spit and swallow. Fragments of food choked her, while other pieces flew from her mouth and into the air. She threw out a hand to push them away, further away, then, at the same time, pulled in her hands as if to catch them. Everything was moving so slowly now, so brightly, that she almost felt able to do so.

Connor watched her, alarmed. What the hell is she doing?

She ran forward, straight into his drum-kit, kicking into his bass drum, clutching his cymbals, embracing them, pulling them towards her and then tossing them sideways, like a discus thrower: up, over and against the wall. She fell forward, scrambled forwards, collapsed on to her knees, crawled to the bed, put out both hands to the tray, on to the plate of food and grabbed hold of a fistful of beans.

Tomatoes! she thought. So red, so bloody red and soft and smooth and full of pips and tart.

She rubbed the beans across her cheeks and down on to her neck.

Connor stumbled over the drums, across the room, towards her. She picked up the egg he'd fried, still warm, still soft, pushed part of it into her mouth and the other part she pushed from her ankle to her thigh, feeling it kiss her skin, like a slippery vulva, like the keen, wet lips of a lover.

Connor was standing beside her now, stunned, desperate to say something, anything, but not knowing what.

Sylvia picked up the juice, fresh orange juice with bits of

orange in it, tiny fragments of fleshy, tadpole orange in it swamping the liquid. She inhaled it and squealed, throwing out a hand ecstatically, and finding, blindly, Connor's leg, the coarse fabric of his trousers. She held firmly on to the glass and then yanked herself up, pulling at his trousers, almost toppling him over. Once up straight, she tipped the orange over him, but his clothes swallowed the juice, so she put her hand to the throat of his shirt, grasped it and ripped at it, seeing the buttons pop away like so many tiny white frogs, bouncing from the edge of a pond into thin air.

Under his shirt was his chest – hairless. She rubbed the juice on to it, into it, up his neck, on to his mouth, then pushed her mouth against his to suck it off.

'Oranges,' she said. 'Oh God! Like sherbet, like toothache, like a terrible, terrible aching, like a mouse nibbling at your lips.'

Connor stood still, his arms at his side, terrified. She's eating me, he thought. She's ferocious.

She turned away from him, dropped the empty juice glass and picked up the cup of coffee. He put out a warning hand. 'Don't throw it. It's burning hot.'

She ignored him, inhaled the aroma, smiling widely, and then poured the coffee down her neck, chest and the front of her dress. It was scalding hot but she didn't scream. The coffee was like a cat's tongue, rasping at her flesh, tickling her. *The smell of it! The taste!* She licked her fingers and said, 'I want to swallow it through my skin.'

Connor saw her clothes steaming and her skin redden. He grabbed hold of her, pulled her pinafore clumsily over her head, then her pea-green T-shirt. Underneath she was naked. She didn't seem to care. She bent over, picked up a piece of bacon and pushed it into her mouth. He touched her chest, which was staining a bright red. She swallowed the bacon. Her tongue felt alive. Before, she thought, it was only a piece of damp muscle in my mouth. But now I must use it. I must taste everything.

She picked up the coffee cup again and drained the bitter dregs from the bottom of it, then tossed the cup on to the bed. Connor watched her breasts as she threw the cup.

This is terrible, he thought.

She turned to him. 'Where's the kitchen?' but she didn't wait for an answer. Instead she followed the trail of cooking smells, sniffing them out like a bloodhound, letting her senses lead her there.

She pulled open the fridge. Milk, cheese, butter. In the freezer compartment: vanilla ice-cream. She took out these things and went back to Connor, who was still in his bedroom, bare-chested, immobile. She opened the carton of milk, pulled at the waist-band of his trousers and poured the milk down inside. The milk was cold.

'Stop!' He tried to move away. 'Stop that!'

She laughed at him. 'I can't!'

She threw down the empty carton and picked up the tub of ice-cream, ripped off its lid and pushed a handful of it into her mouth.

Connor's trousers were wet and heavy. He began to unbutton them, but couldn't help noticing as he did so how the skin on her chest and neck seemed even redder and angrier. He stopped what he was doing and instead took the carton of ice-cream from her, put in his hand and scooped some out. He applied it to her throat and her chest.

She enjoyed this sensation: the coldness of the ice and the warmth of his skin underneath it. She pulled him to her. He still smelled of oranges. She pushed her face on to his neck, into his hair and smelled him properly. What did he really smell of?

She felt his hands on her breasts, her back, but they held no ice now, were simply touching her. She whispered, close to his ear, 'What do you taste like?' and took a tentative nibble.

'Christ!'

He jerked his head away, slapping a hand on to the spot she'd bitten. He checked his fingers to see if she had drawn blood. The expression on her face implied that she had. He frowned at her. 'That's dangerous.'

'You taste like tomatoes.'

He couldn't help smiling. 'You've still got bean-juice all over your face, it's probably that you can taste.'

He put out his hand and gently wiped some of the mess from her cheek. She grabbed his fingers and pushed them into her mouth, sucking them, tasting salt and garlic and resin. The feel of her mouth excited him. His trousers felt strange, though, as if prematurely full of creamy semen. He wanted to take them off but was embarrassed by his sudden state of arousal.

She sucked his fingers and then his hand, covering it in speculative licks and nibbles. He was being savaged by an irrepressible toy dog. She ran her nose from his wrist to his armpit, savouring him, chewing at his underarm hair and tasting the nasty bitter taste of his deodorant. She spat and screwed up her face. To quell the taste she grabbed hold of the pat of butter and bit into it. He said, 'Don't eat that! It's butter! Don't eat butter like that,' while he tried, at the same time, to pull off his trousers. She watched this and laughed when she saw the head of his penis jutting out from the opening in his boxer shorts. Roughly she shoved him backwards, on to the bed. Her mind was crammed full of buttery things, yellow things, oil and excess.

He lay on the bed, at once hopeful and hopeless. She knocked the remnants of the tray on to the floor, picking up some mushrooms in the process, one of which she pushed into his navel, then straddled him, low down, squatting either side of his knees and staring at his manhood.

She had never seen a penis before and was both fascinated and amused by what she saw. He looked like a pink leek, a radish, a red asparagus. He smelled milky.

His eyes widened as she leaned forward and took the tip of him into her mouth. She said, her mouth now full, 'You taste like an oyster, like a prawn.'

She was not overly impressed by the taste, but it seemed a natural enough flavour so she pressed down her teeth, ever so slightly. He sat bolt upright – 'Don't bite it! Please God!' – and jerked her head away.

He saw her face, so stupid, so child-like, so full of impulse, and wondered what they were doing, what they could do. At the back of his mind he knew that he would make love with her, if he could, but he didn't know, couldn't be sure, that she wouldn't change her mind half-way through, get bored or get angry. She wasn't emotionally consistent.

He pulled her closer to him and touched the redness on her chest and neck, then took her nipple into his mouth as she sat astride him. She pulled it away. 'That's my job.'

Is she joking? he wondered.

Her face was serious. 'If we have sex now . . .' she frowned, 'will it be interesting? Will it taste of anything? I mean, what would we do?'

Even as she spoke, he felt himself diminishing. He said, 'I suppose the point is that you do it because you want to be close to another person.'

She pulled back slightly and stared at him. His face was covered by his hair, his body was lean. Like the bacon, she thought, not too much fat on it.

She pushed his hair away from his face. Underneath it, his eyes were uncertain. She liked that. She felt herself warming inside, bubbling a little, like milk before it boils. She pushed him gently down again and pulled off his shorts.

This is a real, live, proper man, she thought, delighted.

She pulled the covers over him, as though tucking him up for the night, scooped another mittful of ice-cream from the tub, and then slipped in beside him. She pushed down her creamy hands and took hold of his now somewhat flabby member. He gasped at the coldness of her touch.

'Where does this go?' she asked quietly. Then added, 'Don't tell me, I'll guess.'

Where was Sylvia? Out. Already?

Ruby collapsed on the sofa. The dog had been locked inside all day. She'd have to take her out soon. She didn't move, though.

In the kitchen, Buttercup sat under the table, her nose peeking out between two chairs. Close to the sink was a large puddle of urine. The kitchen smelled strongly of dog.

Ruby surveyed this scene, then squatted down and spoke directly to her: 'How can I be angry with you?'

The dog stared back at her, blankly.

She pulled out a chair and sat down on it. Her mind was clean and empty.

Steven had booked them into a small hotel within walking distance of the bridge.

At four they'd completed their sound-check in the club. At five they had a light meal in a tiny café, close to the hotel. At six Brera got up to order another pot of tea.

Sam and Steven watched her as she strolled over to the counter.

'Excited?'

Sam had been staring after Brera, not really concentrating. 'Pardon?'

'I asked whether you were excited.'

She shrugged.

'You've been quiet.'

'Yeah.' She looked down at her hands.

Sometimes she hated being away from home because things could so easily spin out of proportion. At home everything was balanced by a kind of regularity: possessions, routine, family. But when you were away, stupid, small, tiny impulses, thoughts, notions, could take over and dominate everything. She couldn't stop thinking about Sarah. About herself and how separate she felt.

Steven was staring at her, as though expecting her to say something.

She said, 'Did you get to meet my friend Sarah the other day?'

He considered this question for a moment and then shook his head. 'I don't think so. Why?'

'No reason.' Sam focused on his tie – a bright, wide, ugly thing. 'I just wondered.'

Ruby gazed at the dog.

'Dog,' she said eventually, 'You are not enough.'

She stood up and strolled around the flat. Eventually she arrived outside Sylvia's door. Inside, when she listened carefully, she could hear a combination of low clucking and cooing, a deep, meditative humming and a whirring noise. She leaned her body against the door, submerging herself in these sounds. After several minutes she reached inside her jacket pocket and took out a bunch of keys. The metallic jangling that they made and the noise of steel against steel as the key turned in the lock jarred on her nerves. She pushed the door open and stepped inside.

The smell was terrible, but she didn't mind it. She accepted it. Inside the room were birds, birds, birds. Everywhere, like feathery wallpaper, glued to their perches, silent, watching. In the dusk their faces glowed. It isn't dusk yet, she told herself; just seems that way.

She walked over to Sylvia's bed and sat down on it. So many eyes watched her. Why don't they fly away? she wondered. They should do. But they didn't.

Something was tickling her. For a moment she thought it was a feather in her nose, in her throat, but then she realized that it was love. *Love.* An infinitely soft fur-ball of enchantment, an amiable, intimate contentment.

She lay down on the bed and closed her eyes. When she'd closed them, she remembered a dream: a bird at her window and the red sky. A thought floated into her head. *All these things go on, and you don't even notice, but they go on anyway.*

She felt something soft and scratchy on her hand, heard the buzz of tiny wings, the fan of feathers. One by one the birds surrounded her. Some of the smaller ones landed on her arms and chest, balancing on the landscape of her body.

Eventually a small sparrow alighted on her nose. She wanted to laugh and to twitch, but did nothing.

I am so flat, so empty, she thought, and felt suffused with joy.

Connor stroked her cheek, leaning over the bed. She opened her eyes and saw that he was fully dressed. He said, 'I'm going out now. We've got a gig in West London. You're welcome to come along and listen.'

What is this? she thought. I don't want anything else from him, apart from what I've already had.

She rolled over, sniffing the pillows, appreciating the smell of his hair on the cotton covers. 'Go. I've got things to try.'

He didn't really want to leave her. Tonight, he decided, I'll do something by Big Star as an encore, something from *Sister Lovers*.

He said, 'I'll dedicate a song to you.'

'Will you?' She didn't sound particularly interested. 'That's good.'

She closed her eyes. 'See you, then.'

What would Sam think of all this? he wondered, and then realized that he didn't actually care. Sylvia's indifference amused him. Her passion amazed him. These two things balanced each other.

She heard him leaving the flat. 'Come and listen' she thought contemptuously. The fool!

She wanted more than that, and she would have it.

Vincent was icing a cake. Ruby's tiny kitchen was covered in flour and sugar.

He had decided around lunch-time, in a moment of boredom, that baking Ruby a cake would be almost as good as apologizing. Easier, certainly. He couldn't really understand what it was that he should apologize for, so the cake served a dual purpose, was an evasion, of sorts.

He told himself, as he baked, that any sort of relationship between himself and Ruby was impossible. The main problem was that he liked her too much. She deserves worse, he decided, someone who cares more about stupid things. Someone who isn't independent, and who doesn't respect her.

The stage was small and cramped. As they plugged in their guitars and adjusted their microphones, Sam thought wryly, The problem with being a middle-of-the-road band is that your audiences are middle-of-the-road. She considered this for a second and then decided that a short while ago it wouldn't have bothered her, but now it did.

They started their first song after a perfunctory introduction from Brera and an even more perfunctory round of applause from the audience.

Sam squinted out, beyond the lights, at the crowd. How many people altogether? she wondered. Sixty? Seventy? Some sat at tables, but the majority milled around over by the bar. Mainly men.

Sam was glad that they had dressed down. She looked over at Brera, who seemed cheerful enough, her cheeks slightly pink, her mouth singing and smiling. The light that shone on them – two spotlights from above – was filled by swirls of cigarette smoke, as though all the cigarette smoke in the entire place was funnelled into these two bright tunnels. Sam tried to make this halo of light, this nimbus, the edge of her consciousness. She didn't want to see beyond it. She felt as though her mind was programmed to transfer everything before her into nastiness, obscenity and ugliness. She tried to tell herself, But it's my mind that does that. It isn't actually the case, it's only me.

She strummed vigorously on her guitar and harmonized.

The next song started. What we're doing . . . she thought, it *is* right.

She glanced over at Brera again and Brera caught her eye and grinned. But in glancing, she caught several other eyes. Some people, close to the front, were watching her intently, their eyes cutting into her.

She peered down at her guitar, focusing on her fingers, imagining for an instant that her hands were strumming not the instrument but her own body: calming her, relaxing her.

I've never been afraid of performing before, she thought, and then, seconds later: At least, not of being watched. I don't mind people staring. People always stare.

She looked up and out at these people, stared back, but it didn't feel right. It felt as if she were offering an invitation. It felt promiscuous, like responding cheaply to a cheap proposition. She focused on the stage, at a space just in front of her feet.

The point of a performance, she told herself, is that you have to be secure in your own world. You have to show the audience your world, your confidence, your self-containment, and they should appreciate it. They should respect it.

But what was her world? Who was she? She was different. No wonder they stared. The only black woman here.

The song ended and several people clapped. Brera leaned over and said, 'Let's do something light, something funny. This lot could do with cheering up.'

'No.' Sam pointed with her foot at their song list, which was stuck to the bottom of an amp. 'Let's stick with it.'

After a short pause they started to play again.

She's really trying, Sam thought desperately; I can't let her down.

She looked up, focused her eyes and tried to smile. She caught the gaze of one man, standing close to the bar, and realized that he was staring at her breasts. Only at her breasts.

He knows that I'm here with my mother, she thought primly, and it doesn't make a blind bit of difference.

In that instant she doubted everything that she had previously established, in her mind, about the two of them: the show, the act – two women, a mother and a child, taking a stand. Ideas don't translate into life, she thought. Marxism, monetarism, conservatism, communism, feminism. Things can't translate because people are stupid. They won't believe.

She stared at the man by the bar and tried to communicate her anger, her sudden hatred. But he didn't notice *her*, only her body. She sang automatically, she played automatically, but all the while, inside her, a private mantra repeated itself. *I have to carry on. I have to carry on.*

This was Sarah's fault. She knew it. Why am I so bloody suggestible all of a sudden? How can I let her get the better of me?

I have to carry on.

It felt to Sam as though her mind had opened up, like a flower. It was a strange and terrifying sensation. Usually her mind was closed, had one small door and a door-keeper who carefully selected the things that would be let in and the things that would be left out. But suddenly the door was wide open, and the supporting frames were cracking, crumbling, letting in more and more light, more and more air. And *people*.

She closed her eyes, continuing to strum and play. Now she could only imagine everyone watching her, but imagining was bad enough. She knew that simply not caring was a solution, but she did care. She did care and she couldn't stop caring.

Life is a terrible violation.

One song.

Life.

Another song.

Terrible.

The last song.

Violation.

She opened her eyes and turned to Brera. 'That's it. Let's go.'

Brera scowled. 'Not even an encore?'

'Let's go.'

She jumped down from the stage, into the crowd, using her guitar to keep people distanced, stumbled through the club, beyond the bar, out of the exit and on to the street.

She breathed in the night air, looking up at the sky but seeing only clouds.

Brera was behind her.

'Stage fright,' she said, sagely.

Sam wanted to disappear, but couldn't.

When Ruby came to it was dark. The room was empty. The birds had flown. She stared up at the ceiling, trying to establish her whereabouts. Something was bothering her, upsetting her, but she didn't know what. The doorbell rang. She sat bolt upright. 'That's it. The doorbell.'

She jumped up and ran to answer it, hoping it would be Sylvia. Instead it was Vincent, holding a cake.

She pulled the door wide open. 'I was asleep.'

He offered her the cake. She took it and used her free hand to switch on the light. Everything sprang into clear relief. The cake was ineffectively covered in a scrappy piece of clingfilm. She pulled it off, careful not to damage the icing. It smelled of fruit and spice.

'Weird cake,' she said, sniffing it. He pushed past her and

went into the living-room, turning on the light and sitting down on the sofa.

She followed him. 'What's this for?'

He shrugged, smiling. She watched his smile. Could she forgive him? This was his way of saying sorry. What for, though? Which particular thing was he apologizing for? For not fancying her? For nearly losing her her job? For not giving a shit about anybody else?

'I fucked Sarah.'

'Sarah?' she said. 'Isn't she Sam's friend?'

He nodded. 'I fucked her.'

'Thursday night,' she said, feeling sick.

Why had he told her? She stood up, holding on to the cake with both hands. She felt like throwing it at him but thought, No, that'd be too easy.

She walked over to him. 'Take the cake.'

'What?'

'Take the bloody cake!'

He took the cake. He was still smiling at her. He was setting her free.

She walked from the room, down the hallway and into the kitchen. The dog was still there. She looked at her and said, 'I'd forgotten about you.'

She picked up her lead from the table and attached it to her collar.

'Guess what?' she said. 'You're going home.'

She pulled her along the corridor and towards the front door. Vincent emerged from the living-room.

'What're you doing?'

She stopped and turned. 'What does it look like? I'm taking the dog out.'

'Where?'

'Back.'

'Back where?'

Before she could reply he said, 'Don't do that. Don't take her back.'

'Why not?'

'Well . . .'

He thought for a moment and then said, 'She's interesting. She makes you interesting.'

'You're a dishonest bastard. A dirty lying bastard.'

She meant it. She yanked open the door and pulled the dog behind her.

He stared after her, smiling. She was free. He had set her free.

He listened to the noise of her shoes on the tiles in the hall, on the stairs. The tapping of the dog's toe-nails.

When she had gone, Vincent rang for a cab. He was still holding the cake. He considered what she'd said.

There are two worlds, he decided, one in which being honest means something mundane, another in which it means being true to yourself, to real things.

He stared at the cake and debated which world it was that Ruby inhabited until a car horn sounded outside.

I'll take the fucking cake, he thought, getting to his feet; I'll take it.

Sam borrowed Steven's mobile phone in the car on their way back to the hotel. Initially she rang Jubilee Road, but no one answered. Next she tried Sarah.

As she dialled Brera turned and asked, 'Who're you phoning?'

Sam put up a hand to silence her, evading any explanations.

What did she want from Sarah? She couldn't decide. Affirmation? Confirmation? Justification? Sex?

Sarah answered, 'Hello?' Her voice seemed troubled.

'It's Sam.'

'Sam!' She sounded delighted. Sam's heart lifted, but before she could say anything Sarah said, 'She's still in the bathroom. She's driving me insane.'

'Who is?' Sam asked this automatically, not even thinking.

'Your sister. Your mad bloody sister. She's made such a mess. I don't know what Connor was playing at, bringing her here.'

'Connor?'

'Hang on.'

Sam listened. In the background she could hear squawking and

188

splashing: sounds like a gang of children might make in a public pool. She also heard Sarah shouting, saying, 'Do you know how much that costs? A whole bottleful? Do you have any idea?'

After a further pause and more splashing, Sarah returned to the phone. She said, 'I slapped her earlier and she asked me to do it again. She *enjoyed* it.'

'You slapped Sylvia?'

Brera turned in her seat. 'What about Sylvia?'

Sam ignored her. 'You slapped Sylvia?'

Sarah sounded unrepentant: 'Yes. I slapped her and she *enjoyed* it. She asked me to do it again.'

Sam laughed. Like me, she thought. If she slapped me, I'd probably enjoy it too. What a fool. A complete fool.

'You said Connor invited her?'

'He must've. He's out now, though. At a gig or something.'

'Is she OK?'

'Orgasmic.'

Sam smiled. That'd be right, she thought. We are sisters, after all. Something else popped into her head, inexplicably: *It wasn't fear I felt before, only ecstasy*. She knew instantly that this wasn't coherent, but feelings, she decided, like ideas, didn't have to be, weren't *obliged* to be. She said briskly, 'And where's Ruby?'

'Ruby?'

'The blonde woman who's looking after her.'

'Oh.' Sarah paused for a second. 'I don't know where she is.'

Sam endeavoured to take stock of the situation, ignoring Brera's desperate gestures from the front seat.

'OK. Well, thanks for putting up with her. I'll see you.'

'What do you mean? Is that it?'

'I think so.'

She used the cut-off mechanism on the phone and handed it to Brera. 'It's all yours.'

Brera was in a state of intense agitation. 'Who was that? Who slapped Sylvia?'

Sam laughed. 'Someone who should know better,' she said.

*

Shortly after Sarah had hung up, Vincent arrived, demanding money for a cab, clutching, somewhat incongruously, a large iced cake which smelled of apples and cinnamon.

Sarah said, 'Hi,' and made as if to give him a hug, but he put out a restraining hand.

'Hold on. This is precious.'

'Who's it for?'

'Nobody.' He glanced over his shoulder. 'Would you pay the cab? He's waiting outside.'

Sarah went to get her purse. Vincent walked into the living-room and was about to switch on the television when an assortment of peculiar noises captured his attention. They were radiating from the bathroom. He walked in and found Sylvia.

She was in the bath, up to her neck in water. The bathroom smelled like a perfume counter. Sylvia was naked but seemed unembarrassed.

'Hello,' she said, recognizing him from their previous encounter. She sloshed around lazily in the water, grinning, watching as waves of liquid spilled over the rim of the bath and on to the floor.

Vincent tried not to fall over on the tiles; which were now wet and slippery. He held his cake aloft. Sylvia spotted it as she peered over the edge of the bath. She sat up. 'What's that? Is it for me?'

He shrugged. 'I suppose it could be.'

She stretched out an arm towards him. He saw that her hand was covered in eczema.

'You shouldn't stay in there for too long.'

'Sod it. Give me the cake.'

Her face shone out wetly at him: a round, yellow, exuberant moon.

There was something in her that he found suddenly irresistible. What was it? A carelessness? He said, 'No cake until you get out of that bath.'

She scowled. 'Yeah? Is it really worth it?'

He showed it to her. 'Smell it. It's delicious. It's all natural.'

He saw her nostrils twitch and her eyes ignite. She tried to snatch at it and water spilled from the bath in even greater quantities.

'Out,' he said authoritatively, 'out or no cake.'

She turned her back on him. 'I'm not a bloody kid, or a dog.'

He enjoyed this little display. He liked her unreasonableness. He put down the lid on the toilet and sat on it. 'Fine.'

He then said, 'Ruby must be worried about you.'

'Ruby?'

Sylvia considered this for a moment. He smiled at her expression, which was so expressive, suddenly so serious. Eventually she said, 'From now on I'm living only for pleasure.'

He put a finger into the icing on his cake, scooped some off and ate it. Sylvia watched jealously, her mouth watering. She stood up, stepped out of the bath and grabbed a large fistful of it, shoving it into her mouth. It was delectable.

Vincent watched her, offered her the plate to hold. 'Hedonism,' he said. 'You've become a hedonist.'

She ignored this. She didn't understand what he meant. She said, 'Where's this from? I want more of it. Different kinds, different types. I want to build a world out of tastes like this. A life. Something so beautiful, so delicious, completely full of touching and tasting and smelling and seeing.'

Vincent passed her a towel.

'I made it,' he said calmly. 'And I can make more. I can show you how.'

'Right.'

Sylvia was pleased by this notion. 'I'll get my clothes. Let's go.'

Vincent watched her as she padded from the room. His gut tightened. Ruby was cheap, he thought.

He was cheap too. He had to spread himself very thinly.

So much happens here on a Saturday night, Ruby thought, as she walked from street to street through Hackney – from Pembury Road to Amhurst Road to Mare Street, then along this main thoroughfare for a long, long time.

Eventually, outside the Bethnal Green Museum of Childhood, she ground to a halt. The dog had been behaving perfectly pulling on her lead only where appropriate, for the most part trotting amiably at Ruby's side, obliging and obedient.

'Good girl,' she said, squatting down next to her. She stared up at the bright lettering on the front of the museum and thought, Hackney Wick and Bethnal Green. How far between the two?

She decided to take a bus.

After several false starts she established herself comfortably upstairs on a number 6. The dog clambered on to the seat next to her. It was empty up here, apart from the two of them. She stared out of the front window. The scene before her, lit by orange lights, dark but not yet properly dark – The city, she thought, is never really dark – seemed inexplicably grand. The dog sat beside her, also watching, but her eyes saw things differently, saw everything in monochrome, like fragments of an old film, every detail rendered stark and formal.

The dog sat next to Ruby like another person, upright on the seat, her legs tucked under her, her back ramrod straight. But with every unexpected jerk she fell forward, sometimes only a couple of inches, but other times almost crashing into the window, on to the floor. On these occasions Ruby tightened a possessive arm around the dog to save her from falling, from injury. The dog was too big, too bulky and unsuitable. Like so bloody many of the things in my life, she thought, and then instantly dismissed this idea. Instead she decided, My life is too *small*, that's the problem. Maybe I'm too small.

She tried to map out in her mind the basic constituents of her immediate future. I'll take the dog back, I'll leave her there. I'll return to Soho. I won't see Vincent again.

These were all things she could imagine happening. Also, though – and this was the wonderful part, the amazing part – she could imagine, just as easily, these same things not happening.

Sometimes, she thought, you can get on to a bus and the bus driver forgets to stop, or he loses his way, or he has to change his route because something unexpected happens – roadworks, or a traffic jam, or a flood – and then everything is changed; because of that, everything is different.

She relaxed and smiled to herself. In life, she decided, there's an outside and an inside. Things happen outside and things happen inside your body, inside your mind . . . ideas, decisions, feelings. Happiness is just a question of balancing the two.

The bus stopped abruptly and the dog fell forward. She caught hold of the dog, falling forward too.

In that split second – as she moved through the air, hearing the bus's horn and the squeal of brakes, feeling the dog's ribs, her fur, her breath – in that tiny dart of time her mind became a microscope. It took in everything, and every detail was significant.

This could be the beginning of something immaculate, she thought.